★

Was everyone in this place in on it? A vast conspiracy to remove Orville Sampson from this world? Why else should they be so uptight about my investigation?

The funny thing was, when I saw the gun, my first thought was not fear, but how much more difficult it would be with this newest threat to keep my secret identity from Tyranny Rex.

When the young chap waved it at me, smileless, and said, "Move," more or less, I reflected ever so briefly on the impetuosity of youth and quickly decided I would not provide an argument.

My fear shifted: did this whippersnapper know anything about firearms, or was he liable to discharge the doggie in my direction by accident? Or on purpose, actually, the result would be the same.

★

ALISTAIR BOYLE

WHAT NOW, KING LEAR?

W⊕RLDWIDE.

TORONTO • NEW YORK • LONDON
AMSTERDAM • PARIS • SYDNEY • HAMBURG
STOCKHOLM • ATHENS • TOKYO • MILAN
MADRID • WARSAW • BUDAPEST • AUCKLAND

WHAT NOW, KING LEAR?

A Worldwide Mystery/September 2006

First published by Allen A. Knoll, Publishers.

ISBN-13: 978-0-373-26575-6
ISBN-10:   0-373-26575-1

Copyright © 2001 by Allen A. Knoll, Publishers.
All rights reserved. No part of this book may be reproduced
or transmitted in any form or by any means, electronic or
mechanical, including photocopying, recording or by any
information storage and retrieval system, without permission
in writing from the publisher. For information, contact:
Allen A. Knoll, Publishers, 200 West Victoria Street,
Santa Barbara, CA 93101-3627 U.S.A.

Printed in U.S.A.

WHAT NOW, KING LEAR?

ONE

SHE WANTED TO MEET secretly—on neutral ground. Her husband had been murdered and there wasn't any reason to think she wouldn't be next. That was why I sat facing her on the sunny patio of a hotel restaurant in Bel Air—a locale not encumbered by the riffraff—a place whose door I had never, heretofore, darkened.

Pamela Sampson was she. The me is Gil Yates, private investigator. So private I am always astonished to get calls on my voice mail. I'm not listed. And that's not my real name. I had reason to hide my identity, and being named Malvin Stark was just one of them.

Orville Sampson had not been Pamela's first husband. She'd had two more of them—both recognizable names, which my canon of ethics prohibits me from mentioning.

One of Pamela's particular geniuses was to marry rich.

Another reason I hid my identity was my *modus operandi*—a nice, pretentious Latin phrase meaning mode of operation. It was taught to me by my boss and father-in-law, Elbert August Wemple, Realtor, the gas bag's gas bag and the man who wrote the book on pretentiousness.

But at places like this Bel Air patio, some grounding in pretentiousness came in handy.

Pamela had deep dish dimples and wasn't lazy about cooking them up to sauce her wiles. She spoke not so much in sentences as in dimpled ideas.

"Stepchildren!" she said with a flourish of her napkin between her lap and lips. "The bane of my existence. *Especially* Orville's three daughters, *and* their husbands!" She made a face befitting an ill-fitting garment that threatened to cut off circulation to her vitals.

Pamela was eating some kind of lettuce concoction with a vinegary dressing on the side. I put her knocking at the door of fifty, so I was glad to see she was being kind to her vitals.

She wasn't about to sacrifice her svelte figure just because she was a widowed woman. *Especially* not because she was a widowed woman.

I was pleasantly chewing a pastrami on a fat French roll, the delectable juices coursing down my dewlaps.

"One of the kids did it," she said, dabbing a little vinegar from her mouth. "I'd bet my life on it."

"A girl would kill her father?" I asked, thinking of my own daughter, Felicity, and not wanting to believe.

"Well, not with her own hands. That was the thing about Sampson's daughters—they never had to get their hands dirty. Now their *husbands*—they've got hands just *made* for dirt."

"What attracted them?"

"Poor self-images—the poor girls were susceptible to anything in pants that came down the pike and looked at them cross-eyed. Mind you, I don't say their poor self-images were without foundation. To the person, they were losers, and popular cant to the contrary, likes do attract.

"It should be an easy job for you. You won't have to look further than the family," she said, as though a child could have divined that.

When I showed her by frown that I wasn't following her, she said, "Orville put oodles of money in trusts for his three daughters—let's not even talk about if they were worthy of it—now, he *controlled* those trusts during his lifetime. All they had to do was wait until he died and they'd have their grubby little hands on three hundred million or so, but no, they wanted more, sooner. He spent some of the income—peanuts, really, in the scheme of things. He bought me jewelry—he loved to do that." She flashed some diamond rings at me, but I didn't know much about the stuff. They say diamonds are forever, but if she isn't going to last forever, why give her a diamond?

"But what really frosted a couple of them was Orville's political donations to candidates they hated. Well, he *made* the money, after all, if he wanted to give the income to Attila the Hun, what business was it of theirs?

"Orville always said it was easy for his kids to hate his business-oriented candidates because the kids never earned a dollar on their own. Seemed to think the money was their birthright and the man who made it shouldn't be allowed to spend it."

"Any big gifts in the last year?"

"Not since they filed suit. It just killed him. They didn't need the gun and bullet, he was dying of a broken heart. He walked around like a zombie."

"I guess they were never close."

"Close? How close do you get to a man as dynamic as Orville? What attempts did they make? Spoiled rotten." She did something with her nose and upper lip to indicate a bad smell.

"And, hey, Blue Eyes, I'm not trying to tell you he was a perfect father—how could he be when he was out making a billion bucks to put in their bank accounts? Well, I say it was the men put them up to it."

"Are the men the original husbands?"

"No. Second editions—each one. I can't say the firsts were any better. By the time the second courtships were beginning, they'd had their share of drug addictions, weight problems, mental disturbances, depression—the usual problems of the spoiled rich, and those, should I say inconveniences, took their toll."

Pamela looked me in the eye, giving me the feeling

she was doing her own detective work on my trustworthiness. "There was this annoying clause in the will," she said, giving in to my purity of heart. "If Orville died in a crime, the criminal must be caught before anybody gets any money."

Clever, I thought. "But it didn't keep him from being murdered," I said. "Did he tell anyone?"

"Ah, there's the rub," she said. "He didn't tell me, and I'm sure he didn't tell the kids."

Not much of a deterrent, if he didn't tell anyone, I thought. "Didn't help," I said.

"Well, it puts pressure on us to find out. That's why I want to hire you—oh, don't get me wrong, I don't care about the money, I've got a nice allowance from the estate pending, blah, blah. I can stay in the house, travel, do anything I want. No, what I can't stand is loose ends, and this is the loosest. Besides, I can't stand those kids thinking I did it. Well, two of them, anyway; I assume the third knows who did it because *he* did it." She shook her head. "I still can't get used to it: Orville gone—once he was strong as an ox. Indestructible."

"What can you tell me about the kids' husbands?"

"Jason Q. Jackson is married to Francine, the oldest daughter. He was a plumber by trade, and I think they met when he was unplugging a toilet." She rolled her eyes. "Soooo romantic," she said, the sarcasm dripping from her dimples. "He's built like a moose. Of course, now he's an entrepreneur."

"Doing what?"

"God knows. Anything he can get his hands on that has as close to a zero chance for success as you can come.

"Then there's lovely Kurt B. Roberts. You wouldn't think he was a pathological liar to look at him. Quite presentable, really. Short, even in his elevator shoes. He was a chiropractor—he has the annoying habit of putting one hand under his chin, the other on the back of his head and jerking his head to one side in polite society—snapping his backbone with a great cracking sound."

"Does he still practice?"

"Heavens no, why should he? I think they met when he manipulated Lolly's back. It was a tiny step to manipulating her psyche. He's a real estate mogul now—the riskier the venture, the more he salivates. Kurt didn't join the lawsuit—just instigated it, then backed off to ingratiate himself with Orville. Too clever by half. If they win, he benefits. It's a no-risk deal."

"How did the other two meet?"

"Rolf was an auto mechanic. Fixed Brenda's car and her in the backseat—right in the shop." She shook her head. "No accounting for taste," she said wistfully.

"Whose? His or hers?"

"Both," she said. "But that was the thing about the marriages—the men saw the obvious dollar signs. God knows what the girls saw."

"What's the mechanic's last name?"

"Gorberg. Rolf Gorberg."

"What about your husband? What kind of guy was he?"

Her eyes misted over—I thought it was an expression of genuine sentiment.

"I loved him, Mr. Yates. With all I had. He could be an S.O.B., but I saw through the bluster. He came from nothing. I wasn't rich in my youth, but I was royalty compared to him. I mean, my father was a postman and my mother took in washing."

"Well," I said, surprised at the admission, "you've done well—"

"Darn right, I've done well, but I earned everything I got by the sweat of my brow. You know how many women in my circumstances marry wealthy men?"

"No, I…"

"And I've had *three*."

"What's the secret?" I asked.

"There is no secret," she said, "only enthusiasm. I'm sorry… You asked what kind of guy Orville was. Let me tell you a story by way of explanation: We had a serious drought in Bel Air some years ago and the city put in a water moratorium and a fine for anyone who used water in excess of their stringent allotment. Mr. Sampson's fine was thirty-five thousand dollars for the two hottest months. He paid it. 'I like grass,' he said. Grass wasn't the only thing that man liked. He liked wealth, power, women—the order depending on his mood.

"He'd had two prior marriages—both very successful for a couple of years. As he got older, his wives got younger. His employees (there were just shy of eighteen thousand of them) used to joke behind his back that if this behavior kept up, the old man would exit this life in the arms of his twelve-year-old bride.

"He was in the papers all the time. He was a maverick, a buccaneer. Very colorful. He settled three hundred and fifty million bucks on each of his three daughters. Of course, there was a catch. The money was put in trust for the girls to get it out of Sampson's already overburdened larder. It was a tax dodge. Let's say the bulk of the corpus, as the lawyers say, was in tax free bonds. That luscious income would be tax free. And Sampson could have it for his own while he was alive. When he croaked, the girls would get a considerable slice of the pie.

"But now two of the girls, or perhaps, their husbands got a little antsy, as they say, for verily it is said, what good is three hundred and fifty million if you can't touch it, feel it, smell it, or spend it? Besides, what if the old man outlived them? Confucius say more fun to spend money while alive.

"Sampson thought so, too. And he was, if he did say so himself, a world class spender. He was one of those rare birds who not only knew how to make money, but also how to spend it. 'Stimulates the economy,' he used to say—'and also stimulates the hell out of me.'"

Pamela's eyes were awash with tears.

"The unspoken fear here," she said, "is…am I going to be next? I've already caught the vibes that the kids aren't happy with the provisions in the will that include me."

My eyebrows went flying. "Three hundred and fifty million each isn't enough?"

"When it comes to Orville's kids," she said. "Human greed knows no bounds."

"Speaking of greed," I said cavalierly. "Shall we talk fees?"

She waved a hand at me. "Anything you want," she said.

Now I was on the spot. I'd heretofore been sensitive about greed, but if this wasn't an open invitation to excess, I don't know what was.

I pitched a multi-tiered fee schedule starting at one hundred thousand dollars if I found the culprit to five million if he (or she) got the death penalty and ten million if it was carried out. Her getting her share of the estate automatically triggered a one million dollar bonus.

With the mention of each fee level I surreptitiously checked her reaction for apoplexy. Like the plastic surgeon quoting a price on breast augmentation. He says "five thousand," and if the patient doesn't flinch, he says, "Each."

Then I presented to her my fear: If I work on this and the police solve it in the meantime—I could be out quite a lot of time and money. "All the same, I'd feel a lot more like putting my heart in the investigation if I knew I'd be compensated, no matter who got the credit for the solution. The police could solve it based on my investigation so just to keep it friendly and cover my expenses, how does one hundred thousand sound, if the case is solved by the cops after I've worked six months?"

She shook her head. "The police have had eight months. Their trail must be stone cold by now. They are frying other fish. I'm told you have ways the police don't—what was the word he used? Harmless? Unthreatening? Something like that. Said you could disarm the cannons off a battleship or the stinger out of a wasp." She checked me for my reaction.

Blasé. It sounded like a setup to me. "Who recommended me?"

"A mister Harold Mattlock," she said with one eye closed. "I trust you remember him?"

Now I raised my eyebrows. "Indeed," I said. She was talking about one of the richest men in the country, whose life I was instrumental in saving—if I may modestly say so. I told the tale in *The Unlucky Seven*. Leave it to Pamela to hobnob with the mega-rich.

She nodded silently. "You aren't cheap, are you?"

"I never wanted to be cheap," I said. "I'm sure you

didn't, either. I suppose we both realize should one of the children be disqualified from inheriting, their share will go to you, and according to my quick calculation, I peg that share at about two hundred to three hundred million, after taxes. Allowing for compromises and settlement, lawyers fees and what have you, I think I'm being embarrassingly modest."

She smiled in silence, and nodded like a marionette with a broken string. She didn't have to say anything more. She was in the can.

She looked at me square on, and I could feel her getting fuzzy all over. "Are those eyes of yours as blue as they seem?" she asked.

It was a question I am still trying to analyze.

How blue do they seem? To whom? I can't see them. How do you quantify color? All life is perception. What was hers? I expect she was trying to mitigate the fee with all that flirty stuff.

Nonnegotiable.

Still unnerved by her blue-eye question, I decided it was unanswerable, so I asked her, "What surprises will I find?"

She looked at me with a smile on her dimples. "If I told you, it wouldn't be a surprise."

"But it would save me a lot of time."

She frowned in consideration. "Oh, you'll hear unfounded rumors about me and one of the boys. Don't believe them."

"Because they aren't true?"

"Well of course truth is relative, isn't it? And it's all perspective."

I couldn't get any more out of her on the subject.

TWO

IT WASN'T DIFFICULT to see how Pamela Sampson was so successful attracting all those rich men, with that big-blue-eyes blarney. She could look at you and make you think that you were not only the only person in the world, but the only person who had ever mattered.

After lunch, I went back to the office of Elbert August Wemple & Associates, Realtors, where I served my time as property manager to Big Bucks himself. It was part of the package—the other part being marriage to his daughter, Dorcas (I kid you not), whom I affectionately refer to as Tyranny Rex, or Tyranny Wrecks, if you aren't too careful about spelling.

It seemed only minutes after the blessed nuptials wound down that both Daddybucks and Dorcas dear wound up: he into an insufferable boss, she into a rather larger package than I bargained for, with lungs the size of a blast furnace, which she utilized in her glass blowing trade. It was a hobby I found kind of charming in the beginning, until it took over both our lives, our house and our bank account. You might say her glass blowing was what drove me to this contingency investigation racket. I desperately needed some cash and an opportunity to get out of the house. I couldn't stand my job, so it was no use pretending I was a workaholic. Of course, there was my modest but pricey palm and cycad collection in the backyard, and that gave me an excuse to get *out* of the house, it just didn't give me a reason to get *away* from the house.

Those not so auspicious beginnings with Mr. Hadaad, the notorious arms dealer, were chronicled for posterity in *The Missing Link.* Isn't it funny how there are often missing links in life, but so seldom are they the links you want to be missing?

At Elbert August Wemple Ass. Realtors—the abbreviation is too delicious to pass up—we are on the floor of a warehouse that has all the warmth and charm that name implies.

The real estate salespersons, known as top producers—like some prize Guernsey cows—chug away in the back. It is as though their gratifying production, which warms the cockles of Daddypimple's concrete heart by goosing up his ever inflating bank account, earns them the coveted position on the floor—as far from gasbag as is achievable in the confines of that particular dump.

I, on the other hand, am the closest one to the King of Siam. Since I am a salaried employee—if you allow your imagination to run amok with what "salary" implies—and Daddydandruff wants to make certain he is getting his money's worth. But considering the shrunken size of the salary, Wemple, Ass. would be getting his money's worth from a mummy.

"Malvin!" he barked as soon as I sat down. "What the Sam Hill is happening out in Hollywood?"

I'd told him not to touch Hollywood with a ten foot pole, but I realized too late that was tantamount to forcing him to buy at gunpoint.

In answer to his question, I looked nonplussed and gave my shoulders a minishrug, expending the absolute minimum of energy to get my point across.

Daddypimple had on his favorite dark brown suit which showcased his dandruff like no other. For some reason, Daddybucks thought brown was becoming. Personally, I never saw it—but then what was becoming to a guy with dishwater eyes and the pallor of moldy cheese?

"This furniture thing is a ball of snakes," he was saying through my baloney filter which didn't seem to be working. "Come up here, I'm trying to talk to you!"

I hied myself up the steps to his elevated platform and had my usual drink of his cooled water—the water dispenser in back was not cooled. Too expensive— "Let them eat cake," was Elbert August Wemple Ass. Realtor's philosophy.

"Easy on the water," he said as I was tapping my second cup. "It has to last till Wednesday."

I groaned, but not so loudly I would lose my job.

"Yes, well, I didn't intend to go into the furniture business when I bought Afton Place—"

Then why did you buy a furnished building you nincompoop? I asked myself. To him, I just looked dumb. I was good at it.

"Look at these bills! You approve of all this?"

"Manager thinks if you want to rent the apartments for what you are asking, they needed some new furniture."

"Some? This is enough to furnish the Taj Mahal."

"Lot of vacancies," I said.

"Geezus jenny," he said. "Can't you do a little comparative shopping?"

"Did," I said. "That's the cheapest stuff money can buy."

I let him rant. I was thinking of Dimples and her job. Had I been too heavy on the fee? For a change, it was a job I wanted, and not only because of her dimples. It was pretty straightforward. It had to be one of the kids, probably hired a killer, it was only a question of breaking or tricking one of them somehow. And everybody was close—no acrobatic charades would be required to snatch time from my daily drudgeries.

Usually, I could count on Daddydandruff to wind down his tirades in a more or less reasonable time. Not this time. All of his other apartments were unfurnished, and I don't think he grasped the economics of furnished properties—expenses and turnover were a lot higher, so the price to earnings ratio was lower. So when Daddybucks bought the place, he thought he was getting a bargain. He wasn't.

I stood up as his facial color was shifting into a bloodier shade of red. "Where the Sam Hill do you think you're going?" he asked.

"I'm going to check it out, sir."

"Good!" he said. What could he say? I had already stepped down from the throne platform without stopping for another shot of water.

At home Miss Lungs of ought ought was blowing glass in the garage, but I barely looked in as I passed. She seemed to be working on the adorable defecating cow at the moment, forever swelling her inventory of that prolific bovine. Tyranny was well on her way to having the largest inventory to sales ratio in the country.

I went right to the kitchen to call for my messages.

The sink was piled high with dirty dishes, and remnants of breakfast festooned the counters and kitchen table. Dorcas Wemple would never win the Good Housekeeping seal of approval.

There was a message to call Pamela Sampson. I had not expected so quick a response. I, however, did not feel I should respond as quickly, so I went out back to pass some time putzing among my palms and cycads.

I was getting three new leaves on my *Encephalartos latiifrons,* and when you paid two thousand dollars for a plant, that was good news indeed. It only had five leaves when I got it—four hundred dollars a leaf by current mathematical standards, and three new leaves should lower the per leaf cost, but the old ones died, so it was, in the beginning, a matter of holding your own.

My *Arcnontophoenix alexandrae* was showing a couple of brown leaves, but the new spike was green. All in all, the place looked good, as did my new addition next door, at the property I bought with one of my obscene fees. I rent the house out and have already filled the front, back, and side, with palms and cycads. I now have my eye on the house on the other side.

After I had moseyed around both yards, checking out the snaillike progress of these rare, exotic, and painfully slow growing plants, I went inside to return Pamela's call.

Pamela picked it up on the first ring. I loved any sign of eagerness.

When I told Dimples who I was, she said, "You're on."

THREE

PAMELA SAMPSON gave me names, addresses, and phone numbers of anyone she thought would be helpful.

She seemed reluctant to give me information about the detective in charge of the case.

"I'd just as soon you didn't fool with them. They've produced zilch in all this time. They don't even seem interested anymore."

I didn't argue. It would only take me a little more time to get the information myself.

I drew up a contract, she signed it. No playing footsie, no reneging—too good to be true.

Despite her reluctance to involve the police, my first stop was the cops. After the usual rigmarole for a big city force, I got to the detective in charge, Sgt. Keith Wajahowski; the foot soldier's foot soldier.

From the moment I sat at his desk at a barely perceptible nod that I do so, I sensed the Sergeant was thinking of more agreeable things.

I introduced myself and started to explain the case.

"I remember," he said. "Still working on it, off and on."

He was a beefy guy whom I suspected was straining the department upper limits on weight. He had a load of eyelashes that might have overturned a dump truck, given the right slant to the road.

"So, what can I tell you, Phil?"

"Gil—"

"Yeah."

"Pamela Sampson hired me to help out."

"Yeah," he said, nodding. "She gets antsy. Complications with the will, I believe." He shook his head at the memory. "That was some babe. Did she tell you she liked your eyes?"

"Well, I—" I fumbled. "She might have."

"Yeah, me too."

I felt a stubborn weight sink down in my bowels. I thought she had been sincere.

"Have any suspicions?" I asked.

"Sure—her."

"*She* is a suspect?"

"Primo—"

"No! Why would she hire me?"

"Throw us off the scent."

I realized if I nabbed her as the killer, wrangling a fee would be problematic.

"What makes you think Pamela might be…"

"Check out the will. Rumors they weren't as close as they once were."

I could relate.

"Or as she'd like you to believe."

"Nothing on the sons-in-law?"

"Lunkheads to the man. Just don't see any of them having the gumption to pull the trigger."

"Hire it done?"

He shrugged his tough-guy shoulders. "We didn't find anything."

"What did you find on Pamela?"

"Nothing concrete." He tapped his mounding middle with his balled hand—"feel it in my gut."

I didn't feel it in mine, but I didn't have a lot to go on.

"Something about her and that lovely eyes routine. I don't know. Lot of dough there. He'd been married eight years to each of his first two wives and the eight year milestone had passed with her. I say he had an eight year shelf life with his marriages."

"And it had been exceeded?" I asked.

"Yeah."

"No suspicions about the kids or their husbands?"

"Oh, sure, but nothing I can take to the bank. A bigger bunch of ciphers you'd never hope to meet. All well-suited to each other." Those hammy shoulders bounced up again. "What can I tell you? There's definitely more there than meets the eye. My eyes just weren't meeting it."

"Anything unusual I should know about?" I asked.

"Unusual? Yeah, what's unusual. Large amounts of cash were siphoned by Sampson off the trusts. He had a girlfriend, but she was devastated by his death. I have a feeling she had hopes of being mentioned in the will."

"But she wasn't?"

"No—but she admitted to getting a lot of cash from him."

"What's a lot?"

"Oh, he'd take ninety-five hundred out a couple times a week—just under the ten thousand dollar limit where the bank has to report it to the government."

"All accounted for?"

"Well, not exactly."

"How much couldn't you trace?"

"A million and a half, give or take."

I whistled softly. "Blackmail?"

"Considered it of course. But Sampson was just too big—what did he have to cover up, and who cared anyway? The golden age of blackmail is behind us," he said. "Born poor, made a lot of money by taking a lot of risks. Bit of a womanizer." He bobbed his shoulders. "Just couldn't tie it all up. Hard to get a handle on cash."

Was it ever, I thought. Daddybucks Wemple wrote the book.

"You haven't given up?" I asked, hoping he had.

"Oh, no," he said. "Just shifted to the back burner." He smiled ruefully. "Waiting for a break."

"What kind?"

"Oh, nabbing the hit man who wants to buy his way

out by getting on the stool. Someone a hit guy blabbed to. An accomplice—one of the daughter's spouses ratting on another."

"Were they that close?"

"Not that I could tell, but you never know," he said. "Murder makes strange bedfellows."

He wasn't a lot of help, but it was a start. He had changed my thinking on Pamela.

Sgt. Wajahowski offered to save me a little time by letting me photocopy anything I wanted from his file.

I thanked him, and he said, "Anytime."

But he didn't mean it.

FOUR

Time to take the gloves off with Pamela Sampson. Time for some hard questions. I wasn't about to do any hubcap spinning if I thought she was the culprit.

Driving up the driveway that might have benefited from mileage signs, I saw more grass than I'd seen anywhere outside a golf course. And it was *perfect,* not a weed as far as the eye could see. I saw a handful of the horticultural corps puttering around the fringes of the grass. I imagined a gardening staff the size of an infantry battalion.

As I saw the house the size and imposition of a movie screen mansion peeking up over the horizon, I checked my gas gauge to see if I had enough in the tank for the return trip.

Pamela herself greeted me at the door, which I found flattering.

I don't know why Pamela put me in mind of one of those glamour girls of the fifties: the misty, faux blonde hairdo, the big, round genuine pearl earrings, the one hundred thousand dollar necklace with enough pearls to saddle a horse.

The hair was generous, to the shoulders, and gracefully piled and curved, but it was too perfect. I couldn't imagine her sleeping on it—like she'd not only have to remove her hair, but her head, too.

As she led me to the living room, I was amazed at how she moved with a lilting motion, while her hair didn't budge—*plastico*.

As we sat facing each other in front of a friendly fireplace, out of one of those upscale, rustic ski lodges, I made a quick calculation comparing the acreage of carpet in the house to the acreage of grass outside. Conclusion: a tossup.

Pamela trotted out the friendly smile as she folded her manicured hands purposefully in her lap. "So?" she said with a tilt of her cherubic face.

"Well," I said. "I read the will for starters…"

"And?"

"Lot of money, I guess, split pretty much four ways. Not a lot of charity."

"Orville wasn't the charitable sort."

"Did it ever occur to you that the tone of the thing might be adversarial—like pitting you beneficiaries against one another?"

"Duh," she said as though I were an idiot—which, incidentally, was a notion I cultivated. It was when suspects got cocky that they let down their guard.

"Orville *was* adversarial. He liked to pit us against

each other—got a kick out of the squirming and screaming."

"What kind of relationship did you have with his daughters and their husbands?"

"Hardly any. I was able to smile when I couldn't avoid being with them. They had a harder time of it."

"Why do you suppose…?"

"They knew I saw them for what they were—whiny, grasping, intellectual and emotional pygmies."

"So you're saying he's giving each of his kids—and you—three hundred million in cash, and he didn't have anything to do with them?"

"Little as possible," she said. "He didn't mind giving them the money, he just didn't want to talk to them. A little schmoozing might have saved him that lawsuit."

"Not to mention his life," I said.

"Goes without saying," she said.

"You know the police consider you a suspect—"

"Oh," she waved a row of fingers in dismissal. "Everyone is a suspect to the cops. Shooting men is not women's work. I'm sure if I ever tried it, the bullet would go into me. Besides, I told you, I loved him."

"Did he still love you?"

"To the best of his ability," she said. "Remember, he was a very rich and hyperactive man. He wasn't any wimpy house husband."

"Any affairs?"

"Ha!" She let out a shot that pinged like a bullet ricocheting off her largest pearl. "I would be surprised…if he didn't." She shrugged. "Boys will be boys—that's how I started with him, and I always realized deep down how it could also happen to me. No, Mr. Sampson was Mr. Testosterone. It was just part of the package."

Hm, I thought. What a liberal sounding outlook. In my humble experience, however, I didn't know many women who actually felt that way. Was it a smokescreen?

"What would the kids say about you?"

"Oh, probably that I was a jealous shrew. Certainly, it would be to their advantage to remove me from the will—"

"And to your advantage to remove them?"

"Why? Three hundred and fifty million is not enough? This whole house is too much, and I'm getting it."

"And you are getting other property?"

"Oh, yes. All of it. I'm very flattered, but what am I going to do with two thousand apartment units? I'm a girl who could be happy in a condo on the beach. Three hundred and fifty million in cash, another, what? five hundred million in property? I should kill my dear husband to get at staggering wealth I don't even want? How much can you spend? How many cars can you drive? How many places can you live?"

It sounded too good to me. I liked her and wanted to believe her—my fee was dependant on it.

"Why do you think the police haven't solved the case?"

She shrugged. "Bureaucratic inefficiency? Laziness? A clever murderer?"

"Who do you think did it?"

"I honestly don't know. And believe me, I'd love to hang it on any of those deadbeats, or all of them, I just can't figure it out. I'd say they did it together, but they barely speak. Oh, they're all greedy, grasping little agitators, but I can't see any of them having the wit to bring it off so successfully."

I thought *she* certainly had the wit to do it. Another blow against our side. "How did it happen?" I asked her. I'd read about it at the time—the media having a ghoulish fascination with calamities and degradation of every stripe. But I wanted to hear her version.

"He was in bed, asleep. They shot him like a coward. If there's one thing Orville wasn't, it was a coward."

"Where were you?"

"In my bed—we had separate bedrooms—oh, we got together for *that*. We just wanted our own space."

"By mutual agreement?"

"Oh, yes. I'd say so," she said in a manner that gave me doubts.

"How about a thumbnail on the kids and their spouses?"

"Where to start?" she said, looking at the ceiling for help.

"Who is most approachable?"

"Oh, I suppose that would be Jason Q. Jackson. Huge, ever ready smile on his face. Weighing in at twenty-one stone—a sumo wrestler." She wasn't British, but she didn't mind pretending to be. "He was a lot thinner when he was a poor plumber—a man who plumbs the depths of the cesspool.

"But that perpetual smile belies the restless turmoil within. He married the girl, frankly, for her money—and now he's got the girl, but not her money. It rankles.

"He is larger than Orville and me put together, larger than both his brothers-in law—and their wives."

"Why is he so big, do you suppose?"

"I wouldn't say it's so much appetite as a total lack of self-control and discipline. He was a more normal size when he married Francine, but once he had the means, the floodgates just opened up. I mean, understand Francine is no beanpole. They both love rich foods, desserts, and sitting on their fat cans. I think the most exercise either one of them gets is pressing the remote control button on the TV."

"And the others?"

"Kurt is also approachable—but devious. Coming to think of it, all of the girls have married devious bastards. I expect that tells you something about them."

"What?"

"Gullible, easily led, manipulated. Kurt is the master of manipulation. He's the runt of the litter—in the double sense of the group of birthlings and trash lying about."

"Don't care for him much?"

"I won't argue that. But then, I don't care for any of them," she said. "There isn't one of them who can live within their means."

"What are their means? Don't I understand that was the root of the problem? They all have this money and can't get at any of it?"

"No," she said. "The girls also have maintenance trust funds."

"Maintenance? For broken washing machines?"

"Hardly." She smiled wryly. "To maintain them in what, to them, is a basic, minimal fashion. To anyone else, it would be luxury."

"How much is it? Do you know?"

"Not precisely. He gave them each a million dollars for a house, bought them all cars every three years—anything they wanted under one hundred grand. Of course, they could have had a Rolls if they paid the difference."

"Any of them do it?"

She snorted. "As they say in the old country, 'Not bloody likely.' Then he gave them so much a month from the income of their trust funds. Around ten thousand, I believe."

"They wanted more?"

"Ah, yes. They have this astonishing capacity for spending. Inherited it from their father." For some reason, she found that amusing. "Ironical," she said as though she had read my mind and wanted to correct me. "But in fairness, when you saddle yourself with such high ticket items, the costs of maintenance go through the roof. Taxes, insurance and upkeep on a million dollar pad eats into that generous stipend. My guess is the basics, including gas for their gas guzzlers, is around twenty-five to thirty grand the annum."

She had such a clever way of speaking.

"This is without food and the servants they all seem to need to keep up appearances. Very important to kids of their ilk."

I made some calculations. I could see how they could get pinched—and I doubted any of them had the slightest affinity for cycads.

"Do you think they will see me—without me having to resort to subterfuge?"

."I expect they will," she said. "If you use the fool-proof approach."

"What is that?"

"Tell them your hunch is that I am the killer and you are collecting evidence. They should fall all over themselves feeding you dirt."

"That's okay with you?"

"Whatever it takes." She shrugged.

FIVE

PAMELA HAD WRITTEN the particulars: names, addresses, phone numbers—down on a sheet of one hundred percent cotton Crane's bond stationary with her name delicately and tastefully embossed on the top:

Pamela Sampson

No maiden name, no prior married name. Orville Sampson was the richest of her three husbands, though not the most famous. One had been a high profile ambassador who had been rewarded for his openhanded generosity to the Democratic party. He held a number of positions in the government that didn't require a lot of smarts. He carried them off with aplomb thanks to the comfortable cushion of inherited wealth he kept about him.

The second made his bundle in the media after inheriting a modest number of enterprises from his father. She had a knack for pleasing older, successful (that is *rich*) men.

Orville Sampson was her first self-made husband.

I turned that self-effacing car of mine toward Mandeville Canyon and the abode of Jason Q. Jackson and his wife, Francine. According to my cheat sheet, Francine had two daughters by a previous alignment, and Jason Q. Jackson's loins had been without issue. I was not to ask why Francine's ex had custody of the girls. I didn't have to.

There were some fairly modest houses in Mandeville Canyon, but the Jackson house wasn't one of them. It sprawled all over the place, pasted into a hill with beaucoup decks cantilevered to a fare thee well. There were so many trees, I don't think they ever could have seen the sun inside the house.

I left my tires on an asphalt pad that was thoughtfully placed for visitors, and went to the door.

Francine opened it and filled it simultaneously. If you like your chicks wide and formidable, Francine is your cup of coffee. Jumbo cup. She wore glasses without the rims, had a nose like a wisdom tooth, and gray eyes that looked just over my head when she talked, which wasn't that often.

She looked a little weary when I stated my business.

"Will it never end?" she asked, half as a question, half in resignation.

"I hope so," I said. "That's why I'm here."

"You're here at the behest of Pamela, aren't you?"

"She hired me," I admitted.

"Be better off investigating her," Francine said.

"I am," I said, brightening, as though she had pushed a secret button. "Can you help me with it?"

Francine wasn't convinced. "Yeah," she said, with a flat tone that sailed over my head with her gaze. "Well…you can come in…I guess."

I followed her into her cavernous house, which was a sacrilegious mess. The first thing I noticed was a glass-front gun case on the far wall at right angles to a long length of glass. It looked out on some sad Eucalyptus trees bunched together at random.

The gun case was packed with—what else?

We were on our way to some seating possibilities when man-mountain Jackson appeared from one of the satellite sections of the manse. To say he was twice his wife's size wouldn't do him justice. He must have gone through the doors sideways.

"Oh, Jason," Francine said as though she were surprised to see him. "This is a man who is investigating for Pamela. I'm sorry, I didn't get your name."

I opened my mouth to say, "Malvin Stark," my real-world name, and caught myself just in time. "Gil Yates," I said and stuck out my hand for Jason Q. Jackson. He took it with relish and gave it a stylized pump.

He had a dazzling smile that never seemed to leave his lips.

"If you're working for her, you can't possibly be objective—why should we talk to you?"

I shrugged. "If I solve the case, you get your

money. What harm can it do you?—unless you pulled the trigger."

He seemed to consider that, as if trying to remember if he had pulled the trigger or not. He nodded once, then looked around for a place big enough for him to sit.

He found a loveseat that was covered in what must have been Francine's taste with little flowers, frills and doilies. He filled it side-to-side, top-to-bottom. Sumo wrestler meets Martha Stewart.

Francine sat more sedately in a wing-back chair with companion fabric in stripes. That left a twelve foot sectional couch for me.

"I want to tell you right now, I hated the bastard," Jason opened his ten-gun salute. "I'm not a bit sorry he's gone. The stuff he put his kids through made it jus-tifiable homicide."

"So you killed him?"

"Nah, not me. Wasn't anywhere near the place when he died." He was making it easy.

"Where were you?"

"Right here at home—" he looked over to Francine who nodded dutifully.

"Any theories?"

"Lots of them. The S.O.B. put that cute clause in his will keeping the money from us until they find his killer—"

"Why do you suppose he did that? Did he expect to be killed?"

"Must have crossed his mind." He smiled.

"What are your theories?"

"How much time do you have?"

I put my palms up. "Much as you have—"

"That third wife of his is a piece of work. Orville *finally* caught on to her. She was about to be dumped from his will. She knew it. Bam!" He smacked his ham hand into the other palm—something akin to the detonation of a nuclear bomb.

"Think she shot him?"

"Know anybody with easier access?" he asked without compromising his smile. "All very neat. Done with a silencer. She claims to have slept through it. Didn't hear anything." His contorted face left no doubt about what he thought of that alibi.

I must have inadvertently glanced at the gun case, for Jason cut right in and said, "I collect guns. A passion, you might say. Oh, don't worry, the cops have checked them all out. None of them put a bullet in Orville. Be pretty stupid to waste him and put the gun back in my case."

"I think I'm missing something," I said. "Most people might feel that three hundred million was a generous gift, no matter how you cut it. You seem to feel otherwise."

"Orville's mistake was settling all that money on the girls," Jason said. "Naturally, we thought we had all that money, then just as suddenly, wham! we didn't have *any*. You can't do that to people. The idea was generous, all right, but in practice it was just a tease. Turned out it was just an IRS scam. He had no intention of actually giving us that money."

"You mean there was no communication about the trusts?" I looked at Francine. She shook her head severely. She reminded me a bit of my fourth grade teacher who took life very seriously.

"Several hundred million dollars and he didn't tell you about it?" I phrased the question to make Orville the heavy.

Francine shook her head again. "Orville was not what you'd call a great communicator. Putting three hundred million in our names was easier for him than talking to us about it."

"So I guess he didn't intend you to actually *use* the money?"

"Funny way of doing things," she said with a snap of her trap.

"How did your sisters react to the money?"

"They were excited, naturally, until they found out Orville was keeping control. Then they were ticked off."

"So you think one of them—well, one of you, really, might have done it to get the money?"

"Oh, hey," Jason said with a boom box voice, "I thought about it more than once myself. Lot of dough." He looked at his wife. "We could use it around here."

She nodded seriously. "Seriously. But," he sighed as though in regret, "I didn't have the stomach for it."

"Any of the others have harder stomachs?"

He raised an eyebrow the size of the Brooklyn Bridge check out. "Kurt and Rolf. Hard cases, both of them."

"Kurt and his wife weren't party to the suit to get control of the trusts, were they?"

"No—that's Kurt. Let us do the dirty work—then take the benefits—without having to lift a finger. That way he could stay in Orville's good graces. Kiss his rear like he always did."

"And Pamela's—" Francine said with pursed lips.

"Yeah," Jackson said with a resigned nodding motion.

"Could Kurt have killed Orville?"

"Oh, you bet. That's his style, sneak up on a guy when he's sleeping," he said. "He's a chiropractor. They're like shyster lawyers. Ambulance chasers. They treat accident victims for a percentage of the take. The more they treat, the more they make. Lolly had a whip-lash—that's how she met him. You talk to him, just don't believe anything he says. He's a pathological liar. He's personable and bright, he just doesn't tell the truth. Doesn't know how."

"What about his wife?"

"Lolly?" he said. "A *mouse*. Have to be to marry such a snake."

"What about Rolf and Brenda?"

Jason sneered. "Used to be an auto mechanic. You

know what a racket that is." Jason shifted his weight on the loveseat. Poor loveseat. "You know, Gil, none of us are too sad about Orville. Sticking that clause in the will about not letting us have the money that is rightfully ours." He shook his head—the smile was still in place, but it took on a sad character. "Shows how callous he really was."

"So if you had to pick one murderer?"

"Pamela, no question," he said, and Francine nodded her assent. "Pamela was history, and I don't care what crap she feeds you about being a simple girl with simple tastes. She's become accustomed to the good life, and she wasn't about to give it up without an all out fight."

Francine could well have been the error apparent of the family.

On my way out I glanced at the gun case for luck, then stepped to the wall of windows and looked out. I sensed a freezing frenzy in the room.

"What are you doing?" Jason Q. asked with a bite.

"Oh, just admiring your backyard."

"Nothing there to admire." The chill cut right through to the bone. He came up beside me, and I can swear there wasn't a degree of body warmth about him. Before I could see much out back I felt him nudge me away from the glass. I didn't fight him—not with the arsenal he sported.

He did pique my curiosity, however, and as I bade

them both a smiley adieu I vowed to snoop around that backyard to see what he didn't want me to see.

I hoped I looked blasé as I drove off down the canyon to the first store I came to with a telephone.

I called Tyranny. I got the voice mail—and left a vague message about being detained.

I found a sandwich shop to kill some time while I kept my metabolism humming, then killed some more time in a bookstore that had friendly hours for insomniacs. I was not one of those, but I appreciated the generosity just the same for I knew going back to the Jackson's in daylight was out of the question. Preferably I should go after they went to sleep and I hoped that was early.

To reward the bookseller, I bought a copy of *The Palms of Madagascar,* which was a lovely compendium of the numerous palms that had been reclassified in the *Dypsis* genus, as well as some *Raveneas* and a few others.

At about 10 p.m. I made my way back up the canyon. There were no lights on in the Jackson's house, and I thought it was my lucky day.

Not the first time I've been wrong.

I parked on the street two houses up from the Jackson's, and looked for a place to get to their backyard without going on their property.

The house up the hill had a long driveway bordering the Jackson's property so I walked up that and thanked the lucky constellations that no dogs were put out at my trespass.

There was a fairly steep hill behind the houses with a depressed stream bed before it rose to the night sky, which sported enough moon so I could see off and on where I was going but didn't spotlight me.

I had no idea what I was looking for, but apparently Jason Q. Jackson didn't want me to see whatever it was. And it must have been at least partially visible from the expansive windows at the back of the house. The tall Eucalyptus trees seemed to block any potential view, so I thought whatever it was must have been between the Eucalyptus and the house, but my careful scrutiny of the area yielded nothing.

Then I heard a noise like a door opening. I ducked behind a Eucalyptus tree and tried to breath deeply without being heard to still my frantically pounding heart. I couldn't see anybody at the house so I thought it was a false alarm. I took a step back to extricate myself from this mess and my foot sank into some soft ground. I looked down and saw the earth had been indeed disturbed. I sank to my knees and began pawing the loose dirt. I got perhaps two feet down when I felt something. Jason Q. was a lazy undertaker. But as I touched whatever it was I got a queasy feeling that shot into full blown nausea—what was I doing? I didn't want to find any dead bodies. That was not part of my deal. I don't know how long I crouched there without moving, but my muscles were starting to ache and I realized I had two choices—cut and run—bring the cops, or bull it through myself. I didn't want the cops and the potential this discovery had to do me out of my fee should they know about it, so I gingerly pawed some more, my heart going crazy in my chest. I think if whoever it was jumped up and said Boo! I'd have expired on the spot.

Not to worry—I got enough of the dirt removed to discover that the buried body was an animal, and it wasn't moving. A few minutes more and I saw it was a dog. Did I feel foolish. Jason had buried his dog and the ace detective Gil Yates uncovered it in the dead of the night with quintessential stealth.

I took a good look at the late pooch, said may you rest in peace and covered it back up. I don't know dogs from Aunt Jemima, but I'll never forget the look of that one.

As I stood up to vacate the premises as we say in property management, a shot rang out and I don't know how long it was until I realized I wasn't dead. Somebody wasn't pleased I'd seen the dog—but could he see me? I couldn't see him—my mood was such that I felt I should play it safe; I didn't move. I waited for the next shot. I don't know how long, every minute seemed like ten years, so after a couple hundred years, I took a gentle step—being careful not to get out in front of the Eucalyptus trees. Somehow I was able to make my way, retracing my steps, back to my car without another shot disturbing the peaceful night air.

I was never so glad to get out of anywhere. How could anyone get so worked up about a dead dog?

SIX

THERE WERE TWO Mercedes Benzes in the driveway of
the Roberts estate in San Marino. The garage doors
were closed, so I couldn't tell what secrets were hidden therein. I wondered if the two Mercedes were in
any way connected to the Roberts not joining the lawsuit against Orville.

The house was one of those overblown mansions that
you wouldn't see in a movie because you couldn't get
the camera far enough away to take it all in. An iron gate
out front, and a couple acres of grass (shades of old dad
and his aforementioned fondness for grass). Any man
who has more grass than Forest Lawn Cemeteries has
to be a substantial member of the community.

A Mexican servant in livery opened the door. She
was dour of face, nervous of eyes. Not the sort of greeting to bespeak any confidence in the household.

Lolly was right behind her. A dark-haired woman
with a smile as nervous as her retainer's eyes.

Lolly had a round face and a reasonably fit body
which she was at no pains to conceal. She, naturally,
excused her appearance, though I was hard pressed to

find fault with it. Sawed off jeans, with perhaps a tad too much left on the cutting room floor. Upstairs was covered with a clingy, baby blue blouse, which showed, to her everlasting benefit, the blessings of nature.

She wore a touch of makeup and two simple ear studs, studded with glittering diamonds.

Lolly was loquacious. "Come in," she said, "won't you come in? Francine told me to expect you and expect you I did."

Lolly was in rather nice shape. She was also a hand twister—in front of what is euphemistically known as a lap.

The twisting didn't stop after we sat on the long and winding sectional couch—I wrote the family penchant for these mile-long couches off as a genetic deficiency.

The decor was out of one of those tony decorating magazines, and Lolly supplied the reason: "We were a decorator house for Diabetes."

I tried to process that in my unschooled brain, without success. No matter, Lolly was only too glad to fill in the blanks.

"When we bought the place, it was what the Realtor—" she pronounced it Real-ah-tor "—called a fixer-upper." Her left hand left her lap enough to stifle a snicker. "It was in shambles, is what it was; that's why we got it so cheap. Just under a million—oh, they were asking more, but Kurt sure knows how to bargain. He told them right up front we'd need several hundred thousand right away for decorating. Well, they sold it to us, then Kurt turned right around and signed up with the Diabetes people for their decorator open house of the year, and we were still in our old place in Pasadena—" she giggled "—our Honeymoon cottage, we called it. Anyway, Kurt makes this deal and they just tore this old place apart. You know what happens—?"

"No, I…"

"A decorator takes a room and, whew, boy, they just go—like all out. So as you can see, you get a showplace out of it."

"And they *give* you everything?"

"Well, everything that's pasted down or screwed in—" she brought the reliable hand up to cover a blush. "Well…you know what I mean."

I looked around and said, "but a lot of this isn't…"

"Yeah, well, like I told you, Kurt could bargain. Well, he went to work on the decorators. Like, most of the stuff that wasn't…attached," she said with a sly you-know-what-I-*really*-mean smile, "was offered to us at cost. But what with all the restrictions Orville imposed on us in the trust and all, we were not flushed with funds. So Kurt reasoned these decorators would sell for less—what with the difficulty they might have unloading the merchandise on someone else—the cost of moving, storing, financing and what have you—so he was able to buy most of the stuff for quite a bit less than they were asking."

"Well, good for him," I said, trying to be ingratiating—he'd probably get on famously with Daddybucks Wemple, my fatuous father-in-law, I thought.

"Gosh," she said, untwisting her writhing hands and slapping them on her bare thighs with a ringing, stinging sound, "I hope you know *we* didn't kill Orville. I mean, goodness, there was all that mess with the trusts, but we weren't suing him. I mean, like, murder is so messy and all, and neither Kurt nor I know the first thing about guns." She put her finger on her lip in a delightful, stylized gesture— "No, guns are the passion of my brother-in-law—oh," she added with a quick breath, "I don't mean to suggest Jason killed Orville or anything."

"Of course not." I was getting adroit at the facile, meaningless phrase. "Any ideas on who did it?"

"Well, goodness, I don't know. Pamela was right there. The rest of us weren't."

"What does your husband think?" I asked, looking around as though I were trying to locate him, which I was.

"Kurt's outside playing with the dogs. He's got three of the cutest Dobermans you ever saw. This is a second marriage, so we aren't planning any kids. My two are too much for him, so we put them in boarding school and summer camps. I think he's trying to train them or something. Oh," she giggled, "the dogs, not the kids—the kids are beyond it." And she giggled again.

"How did you meet your husband?"

"Oh, Kurt was my chiropractor. I was rear ended and I got this attorney who sicked me on Kurt. He was a chiropractor and they have this wonderful program where they get a percentage of the settlement amount. Between him and the lawyer, they take a big chunk, but the beauty of it is if you don't get any money, you don't pay him a cent."

"Did you get any money?"

"Oh yes." Her hand went up to cover her bubbly smile again.

But Kurt must have known he had to marry her to get the real money. "Does he still practice?"

"No," she said, and I may be mistaken but I think she said it with no little pride in that tilt of her head. "He wants to devote himself totally to me—"

And the management of your money, I thought without saying it.

"Lolly, why do you think your father put that clause in his will about not passing out the money if he was killed—until they caught the killer, I mean?"

"Well, obvious, isn't it? He thought someone was going to kill him."

"Who?"

"His wife is my bet. I mean, they weren't getting along like they did in the beginning. I know he was about to dump her."

"He tell you that?"

She wrinkled her nose and twisted her hands. "Just

a feeling," she allowed. "They used to be so lovey-dovey. Lately, they just snapped at each other."

"How was your relationship with your father?"

"Good!" she answered, too quickly and too emphatically.

"Why do you suppose your sisters decided to, ah, file the lawsuit against him?"

"Oh, I don't know. It was so frustrating, having all that money and not having it, you know? They had so many irons in the fire—sure things to make a lot of money, and Orville pulling the reins in, so to speak, just put the biggest damper on it. Even Kurt turned moody," she said, "and he wasn't easy to live with. He just kept pressuring me. Every day it seemed he'd tell me about another deal we missed out on because Orville was so stubborn about controlling our money."

"Did anyone tell your dad how they felt?"

"Well, yeah, Francine did for sure."

"She told you?"

"Not exactly in so many words."

"Just a…feeling?" I asked.

"Well," she said with eyes wide in wonderment, "yeah. She's the one that started the lawsuit. I guess her husband talked to Kurt and Rolf. She thought it was the way to go."

"A feeling—?"

"Yeah, well, I know I say that all the time, but with Kurt—I *don't* know." She seemed to be considering the effect of something, weighing it, testing it, then ultimately rejecting it. "I used to talk to my sister, Brenda—she was a good kid. I just get the feeling that Rolf turned her against us."

"You have any—feelings—about why Kurt turned down the suit? Does he have enough money—or maybe he doesn't care about it—"

"The others think this was his idea to ingratiate himself with Orville. I think he thought Orville might disown and disinherit all of us if we got too uppity with him."

She seemed to drift off with her eyes which floated toward the backyard and some yipping dogs. "Sometimes," she said in a sorrowful reverie, "I think the suit was all we talked about."

There was a painful silence during which I could think of nothing to say.

"Well," I said when I recovered, "I think I'll go out back and talk to your husband—if that's okay."

Her head bobbed up and down like an apple in a tub of water at Halloween. "Okay," she said, but her eyes glazed over and she was no longer there.

SEVEN

A FOOL AND HIS HAIR are soon parted. That's a tough cliché and I may not have it just right, but I'm trying to say I was a fool without conceding my embarrassment.

What do you think when you hear "Dobermans?" Cute little puppies, adorable companions? A lot of tail wagging?

I went to doggie school out in the Roberts's backyard. The sucker almost took my leg off. The moment I stepped outside, he lunged at me as though I were doggie enemy number one.

"Down, boy," came the barked command of his master, who, if I have any power of perception left, was highly amused at my uncovered fear.

"Shark!" he commanded as my shaking increased at the thought of the aptly named dog. Then I realized it! This was the kind of dog I saw buried behind J.Q.'s house. Intelligence I thought I would keep to myself for once.

Shark backed off but kept his eyes glued to me, lest I make a false move and give him just cause for amputation.

Roberts was smiling bashfully. "Sorry," he said. "They're still young. I'll break them of it. Kurt Roberts—" and he put out his hand which I instinctively examined for steel teeth.

I shook Kurt's hand, though I was still in shock. Malvin Stark was on the tip of my tongue, again. I think I said, "Mm…Gil Yates. I'm investigating—"

"Yes, yes; think you can solve it, Yates?" he said.

"I'm leaning toward the wife," I said for instant ingratiation, without taking my eyes from the dog. "What do you think?"

He nodded with a manly nod of one macho hunk who trained and possessed attack dogs. Of course, he was a runt, but the dogs, three by actual count, gave him swash.

He didn't ask me to sit on one of the many garden benches strewn over the grass, thank goodness. I didn't want to be a sitting goose for the hounds. Being a moving target was bad enough.

"Could I ask you to leash the dogs?" I asked, looking around for a cage.

"Oh," he said, "I'll control them—they don't like to be cooped up."

How considerate, I thought, of the dogs. Kurt seemed in a world of his own for a few moments. "Still can't figure," he said.

"What?" I said, thinking he was going to share a clue with me.

"What happened to the fourth dog—" he shook his head "—had four—two pair—thought I might breed 'em. Good money in it." He licked his lips and shook his head. "Dog napping," he said, "probably someone going to get a hundred bucks for drugs."

I didn't say anything, but I wondered if Jason killed Kurt's dog to get back at him for not joining the lawsuit. It seemed a little childish, but then, I didn't see much about any of these birds that smacked of adulthood.

His brow furrowed, as though he were deep in thought. If he was, he was out of his depth. With a nervous eye to the dogs, I (ever so) gently prodded: "Think your stepmother-in-law, Pamela, did him in?"

After due consideration, he smiled, showing all his teeth intact. "Nah, the girls don't like her, but I sort of do. She told me I had nice blue eyes."

I squinted. "Your eyes are brown, aren't they?"

"No more. Blue. Next she's going to tell me I'm tall. And face it, how many women take guns and shoot men in their sleep?"

"One of your brothers-in-law?"

"Nah—what for, money? The guy was seventy-some years old and not in the best of shape. We could have waited."

If they could have waited, I wondered, why did they file suit?

"I heard somewhere you might have been eager to clear up some debts, make some investments…"

"Sure, I've always got my eye out for investments. I made a killing in Honolulu," he said proudly, "before it went sour." He made a face to accompany that unhappy sentiment.

"Any theories?"

"I'd look for a business rival—someone he stepped on on his climb to the top. Orville wasn't a subtle man with the social graces, you know. He was a hustler. It's a zero sum thing—someone wins, someone loses. If you are losing out to Orville all the time, it gets old." He flashed his ready smile and it was engaging. Could a guy so personable murder?

Wasn't Ted Bundy rather long on a weird charm?

I squinted into his eyes, for the sun was in mine. They were brown, but I looked quickly at the dogs and decided they might be blue after all. Maybe Pamela was color blind; that didn't make her innocent—or guilty.

"What's your take on your in-laws?"

"We aren't close," he answered, his attention on the dogs—thank goodness. I had the feeling it was only his devoted gaze in their direction that kept them from feasting on my flesh.

"Think any of them could have killed Orville?"

"Anyone *could* have," he said. "Jason Jackson is good with guns. Rolf Gorberg is harder for me to get a fix on. It's the lion and the mouse out in Rolling Hills."

I squinted, he explained.

"Brenda's a good kid, I guess, but he rules the roost out in that backwater."

I loved to hear him refer to that gated community of multi-million dollar homes in such a derogatory way. True, it was somewhat rustic next to his San Marino location, but still—

"Doesn't Rolf sound like a spooky, dominant male type? He is spooky. I wouldn't trust him farther than I could throw him—and I couldn't even lift him."

"You guys ever get together? Family things?"

"We aren't too good at it. We tried a Christmas last year and it was a flop. The lawsuit was brewing and I decided not to join in and that ticked Jason off."

"Why didn't you join the suit?"

"I got to thinking it sent the wrong message— wouldn't play well. I needed the dough, but I thought it would appear ungrateful or something." He shrugged. "I decided to keep the channels of communications with Orville open."

"And Pamela too?" I said.

"Yes, of course. Both of them."

As though I hadn't baited him enough, I threw in another dart. "Orville took large amounts from your trust funds, I hear. Any idea what he did with the money?"

"I think they know what he did—spent it on his wife—and assorted bimbos."

"That much?"

"Well, I expect he was a big spender."

"If you had to speculate on what happened to a stray half-million or so—?"

"Petty cash to a guy like Orville. That's why we were so upset with him taking our money like that. Seemed to be no reason. I mean, he had money of his own. He put this in trust for his daughters, then he abused that trust. The government makes laws about those things—if you want tax breaks, you have to fulfill certain requirements. It's give and take, isn't it? Orville wanted to have it both ways, and we just got tired of it."

"I guess no one knew about the clause in the will."

"No, but I'm not surprised. He was that way. But it was kind of academic, I think. I mean, you can't benefit from a crime. You can't get money from someone you murder. So, I don't know if he needed that. I think it was just to let us know if anything happened, he'd be suspicious."

"When was the last time you saw Orville Sampson alive?"

"Oh, I don't remember exactly—a while before his death."

"Circumstances?"

"It was a business proposition," he said, and let it hang there like yesterday's laundry.

"What kind of business?" I asked, and my response was a snarling of a dog. Kurt Roberts seemed to have an uncanny ability to communicate his messages of aggravation to his dogs.

"Oh, I had a proposition for him," he said nonchalantly. "He didn't go for it," he added as though Orville Sampson was one big fool when it came to sure-fire investments.

"You argue at all about it?"

"Oh, we may have had some words. I wouldn't call it arguing."

"No raised voices?"

"Oh, you'd have to know Orville. He was excitable. I'm sure I didn't raise my voice."

I wasn't so sure. From somewhere inside, I heard a phone ring, then stop.

Lolly came to the back door and said, "Kurt, your broker's on the phone."

He smiled at the news. It made him feel important.

"Excuse me," he said to me, and he lurched forward as if to leave me stranded in this dog pound.

"Oh, I'll just go along," I said, almost falling over my feet to get out of there.

Inside, I bid goodbye to Lolly with thanks for her time. Across the room, Kurt was relieving himself of a hearty greeting to his broker. He smiled as though he were trying to impress his broker, and he seemed taller.

I was just climbing into my car when I heard something behind me. My first thought was it was dogs, so

I quickly popped into the driver's seat and closed the door before I looked up to see Lolly coming toward me with a worried look on her face.

Since I didn't see any dogs, I lowered the window to be sociable—but not so low a Doberman could lunge through the opening. She spit the words out in a stage whisper, and the tones were frightened as though she felt the dogs bearing down on her.

"Did he tell you about him and Pamela?" she asked me, her eyes bulging with terror.

I had to say he hadn't. "No, what?" I asked.

At that moment the Dobermans came pouring over the vast lawn from around the house—they were growling and snarling as though they were whooping up some enthusiasm for blood soup.

Smiling Kurt was right behind them, calling them off just as they were about to tear the clothes off Lolly's back and maybe much of her pink, succulent flesh in the bargain.

Lolly got the message and turned abruptly from me and scurried back into the house.

Kurt watched her go. He was amused as he smiled at me and waved goodbye as though we had just shared the most wonderful joke.

Lolly had not been amused. Neither was I.

EIGHT

MY NEXT STOP was Daddybuck's stomping grounds on
the Palos Verdes Peninsula. There, in the elite, but rustic gated community of Rolling Hills, lived Brenda
Gorberg, daughter number three, with her second
string husband, Rolf.

I told the guard at the gate I was going to see Daddybucks Wemple, and gave him the address. That was the
first time his residence in this snotty community did
me any good.

The Gorberg's had a one-digit address. I thought
that was the pinnacle of exclusivity. The glass blower
and I had five digits.

The Gorberg's street was named for a horse. Some
day when I get rich I'm going to develop some land
and name the streets for cycads: *Encephalartos tris-
pinosis* Drive, *Macrozamia lucida* Lane, *Dioon capa-
toi* Road—the possibilities are endless. It could happen
any day now—just as soon as there is a Renaissance
in those cute glass figurines of the little urinating farm
boy that Tyranny Rex takes such delight in blowing.

The Gorberg house was a rambling ranch with the

attendant flies and the smell of horses. The yards of stucco were painted beige to fit into the countryside, but it didn't quite work. Somehow, the tint went awry—perhaps just before they ran out of money, and the place looked like a Hershey bar that had sat too long in the sun.

A mouse answered the door. It was Brenda, as advertised, short, wary, and mousey. Like she was always afraid the cat was around the corner.

I stated my business, and then he appeared: sleek, slouched and suspicious—T.S. Eliot's worst nightmare—ready to pounce.

Rolf greeted me in a suit and tie—a bit of an anachronism in horse country.

The suit was gray and the tie blue. You might say his clothes did him justice—the gray matched his pallor and the blue his complexion. I didn't ask if Pamela had told him he had pretty blue eyes. The suit, I'll admit, did throw me off a bit. I kept forgetting Rolf came up through the grease monkey ranks to husband an heiress. I suppose the suit was serving its purpose.

No one had bothered to tell them I was coming. And there were no servants at this address.

Rolf was a creepy looking guy, hunched over not from osteoporosis, but from a mental attitude that made him want to hunch up to camouflage himself from numerous imagined predators, enabling him to spring up in defense at an instant's notice.

"Yesss," he hissed at me as the mouse stepped aside. He was a modern day Uriah Heep with perhaps a dash of Fagin thrown in the mix to insure his self-preservation.

"Gil Yates," I said, sticking out my hand in greeting, as though he were just as normal as the next fella.

He didn't even look at my hand. The ready, even exhausting smiles of his brothers-in-law, Jason and Kurt, were missing from Rolf's kisser. His lips seemed turned in a perpetual smirk.

"I'm investigating the murder of your father-in-law," I said, feeding this fund of knowledge to a guy gorged in that department.

He considered my pronouncement, his look leaving no doubt about his doubts about my suitability to the task, but somewhere in that mushy gray matter he called a brain, something registered that I might serve his interests, and said, "Well, then, come in, I guess—" and he kept a close eye on me as I entered a living room at once vast and vacant of any defining characteristics. There was furniture all right, carpets, drapes, the usual accoutrements you would associate with a home, only it didn't look like a home, but rather a floor display in a horsey furniture store. There was something missing from the picture. Brenda. She had vanished from the room without a trace. It was now the sole and exclusive domain of the man of the house.

I looked out the window to some stables in the back. "You have horses?"

He nodded. "Arabian studs."

"Breed them?"

"That was the plan," he said.

"Was?"

He threw out his hands. "The money is tied up," he said.

"What are your chances of getting the money soon?"

"I should ask you that question. With that stupid stipulation in Orville's will, none of us will see a penny until you or someone else nails down his murderer. Any leads?"

"Just beginning," I said. "Talked to Pamela and Jason and Kurt. And their wives, of course," I said with what I thought a clever jab at his missing wife.

Didn't work. He bristled. "You're wasting your time with that bunch."

"Oh?"

He nodded his sour, sore head. "All together they don't have the combined intelligence of a tsetse fly."

"Not smart enough to murder?"

He looked me over. I'd apparently made the wrong response.

"I very much wish one of them had done it. Boost my share."

"Any possibility?"

"Anything is possible. I guess the kids agree on one thing. All signs point toward the missus."

I nodded.

"You agree?" he asked.

"Partially. I don't think she did it alone—got help?"

"Yeah. You know about her and Kurt—" he was assuming, not asking.

"I'd heard something," I said without telling him how little.

"Hot and heavy," he said, nodding like the sage of Rolling Hills.

"Do you believe it?" I asked, throwing a handful of skepticism into my voice.

"I believe it," he said. "I saw enough—"

"Such as?"

"Oh, the flirty eyes, glances back and forth," he said as though it was putting an unwelcome taste in his mouth. "He used to go over there when Orville was out of town." As if to answer my unasked question, he said, "Lolly talks to Brenda." He looked at me as though I should have found that surprising.

"That certainly puts a different spin on things," I said. "You think they killed him to get him out of the way so they could go on—"

"Stranger things have happened."

"But, geez, isn't she old enough to be his mother?"

"Not quite," Rolf said. "Don't forget, we're talking twice the money and I don't know anyone greedier than Kurt. So what if Kurt *is* a little younger? She's getting more than his wife—besides, there is all that romantic intrigue. Orville played around, she could, too."

"But how do you explain her hiring me to find the killer?"

He looked at me, this creep, as though I'd just said the stupidest thing he ever heard. He looked at me as though the obvious answer was in that look, but when he saw I didn't get it, he felt compelled to explain.

"I don't mean to be indelicate," said Uriah Heep, Mr. Indelicate Incarnate, "but to answer that question, you have to look at who she hired—was it the Pinkertons? Was it any number of ex-cop detectives who branched out on their own? Was it any known entity with a wealth of experience under their belts? Or was it some sweet, harmless guy who—let's just say she thought, anyway—wouldn't know a killer if he fell on him. You're a smokescreen, pal," he said. "And the sooner you admit it, the better off we'll all be."

I suppose the macho guys would let that run off them like a duck sidestepping the rain. Me—it smarted.

"Face it, on the face, she hires a dick to solve the case, it looks like she's clean."

"Suppose I find out she's the killer—"

I saw his first smile—though I couldn't quite be sure, it looked so much like a gastric discomfort. "I personally don't believe in miracles," he said, "but let's say that miracle happens. Do you have any notion that the woman who put a bullet in her husband couldn't put one in you?"

"Occupational hazard," I said with bogus bravado. "Say," I said, bringing my hands down on my thighs to signal a sharp transition in thought, "you think I could talk to your wife—get her take on it?"

His lips clamped together like the closing of an overhead garage door. He shook his head once, but it was so decisively done, once was all it required. "I'm as sympathetic to women's lib as anybody, but one of the reasons Brenda married me was to isolate her from having to deal with unpleasant realities. She's not well. Has this disorder, and I don't wish to see it aggravated."

On the way out, my glances darted furtively about for a hint of Brenda, to no avail. I asked if I could see the horses.

"Horse," he corrected me. I allowed as how that would be sufficient, and he took me through the French doors in the back of the family room, just off the living room, to the modest stable in back.

I know that pride goeth before springtime or something, but if Rolf was trying to hide his pride from me, he wasn't succeeding. He looked at that horse like a lover. He glanced at me to see, I suppose, my appreciation. "Isn't he something?" he said.

"Yesss," I answered, not hiding my ignorance of horseflesh. I'd bet Rolf didn't know anything about cycads.

"You're looking at a quarter of a million dollars," he said. "And the most beautiful animal in the world."

"Does Brenda like horses?" I asked, most innocently. His head snapped in my direction. "This is *my* horse," he emphasized.

"Oh, yes, well…sorry. I just wondered…"

"I could turn this investment many times over, Yates," he said. "If only that capital would free up."

"I'm sure," I said, but I wasn't so sure. Breeding animals was far from a sure thing. We had an apartment manager who tried to make a killing in English Setters, or something, but only got a destroyed couch in the bargain—bitch tried to dig a nest in a brand new couch. Animals were chancy.

"You know," he mused, "it's a ways from my usual work. I worked on cars—the finest foreign cars. The horse was our main mode of transportation before the car was invented. Now I have the finest horse in my garage." He pursed his lips, shook his head, and said, "I've come a long way—"

Backwards, I wanted to say, but of course, I didn't.

I was sorry he followed me to my car. I was hoping for a repeat of Lolly's running out to give me a tip.

But Rolf kept a tight rein on his wife, and I don't think there was such a thing as giving her her head in the big stable in front.

NINE

Zach Nunnaly, Orville's CPA, was not that eager to see me. I cooled my arches for a half hour before he deigned to have me sent into his spacious, but Spartan office.

This guy was as dour as you'd expect a numbers man long in the tooth to be, but he wasn't skinny and bent over in the mold—he was athletic of build, tanned, full head of unruly hair which looked as if it had barely survived a standoff with a mix-master.

He wheezed—not loudly, but often. It was not so much the wheeze of asthma as it was of suffering fools.

He pointed to a chair across the desk. He was saving words.

"You worked for Orville Sampson a lot of years, didn't you?"

He nodded.

"How many, exactly?"

"Exactly? Why, twenty-seven years and seven months when he died."

"Know why anyone would want to kill him?"

He wheezed, then wheezed again. "Why does anyone kill anybody?" he parried with a question of his own. I was glad I came here—I could practice listening to myself talk.

"Oh, there are a lot of motives," I said. I wanted to say, "Choose one," but I was still being careful—"Hate, passion, greed, revenge."

He shrugged.

"So you have no theories?"

"I'm just the numbers man."

"Oh, yes. The numbers. You managed his bank accounts?"

He nodded.

"And the children's trusts?"

He nodded again, this time more guarded.

"See anything unusual, say, the last year?"

"Not really."

"He took out a lot of cash, didn't he?"

"I thought you said, 'unusual'," he said.

"I looked at the kids' records. Talked to Pamela. We can account for a lot of it, but there—in the last six months or so, we have about a mil and a half in cash we can't get a hammerlock on."

I got my first reaction—his eyelids shot up with his bushy eyebrows. I thought the amount startled him, but I should have known better. "A hammerlock?" he said. "I've never heard that expression."

"Oh, yes." I was happy to explain something to this wax-dummy. "It means a strong hold—you know, a tight grasp."

Zach Nunnaly nodded with sage understanding. "Yes," he said. "Get a handle on it."

"That's *it!*" I said with inappropriate exuberance. "So, you have any idea where one million, five hundred grand could slip through the holes in the floor?"

"Cracks," he muttered, wheezing. "Well, you know there were, ah, dalliances from time to time…with women."

I was relieved to hear that. "That expensive?"

He frowned. "Not usually."

"What else could he have been doing that he couldn't pay for with a check?"

He shook his head.

"Gamble?" I asked.

"No."

"Blackmail?"

"A man that rich and powerful is not subject to blackmail," he said.

"Why not? He'd rub the blackmailer out?"

"Destroy him, yes. One way or the other."

"Ever see that from Orville?"

He looked over my head at the far end of the ceiling. "Not in so many words," he said.

"In how many words?"

"I really don't have the information you want."

"Who does?"

"Not sure. Ask around."

"Ask around where?"

He wheezed and looked back at the same spot on the ceiling. "Anywhere. Everywhere...nowhere."

So he was playing the enigma. Did he know something he wasn't telling, or was he just exhaling smoke? He looked me four square in the eye, and then suddenly unloaded what, for him, was a major barrage of information:

"Hey, he made it from the dust of the ground—East Texas is one dusty place. He came out of that dust—bought one piss-ant drug store that was on the verge of closing in the early days of the mega-drug boys.

"So he works night and day at spiffying up that store, cuts the prices so he's running on empty most of the time, but you better believe he's driving those chain boys up the wall. Service with a smile. Comparable prices because now he's bugging the suppliers to death about their prices to him and terms and telling them he's going to own a thousand drug stores someday and he never forgets a favor or the opposite.

"I'm sure you could find a number of those hotshots who would have been glad to kill old Orville, but that was long ago."

"Did he get his thousand stores?"

"He got enough. And when he'd gotten his nice nest egg, he started going after other companies. Tooth and nail, I tell you. Next thing you know, he'd bought another store, then another, like there's no tomorrow. Then he had so many, you didn't know how he could attend to all of them, but somehow he did—driving all over the Texas countryside in his battered old pick up. I came on board early on. Oh, he kept track of the beans in the beginning himself. Used to write the checks and everything himself. Before he knew it, he had a company, he called it Achilles."

"Achilles? Isn't that a strange name—I mean what it means, and all?"

He laughed. "First off, it's high in the alphabet. Second, drugs are about man's vulnerability. Give him something to get him over the low spots. And third, it reminded him how vulnerable he was. Achilles had a soft spot on his heel—Orville kept his heels covered with these god-awful cowboy boots he wore. Liked the extra heft, he said. 'Keeps me on my toes,' he said."

"Someone got through those boots."

"Apparently."

"Any idea who?"

"None," he said, shaking his head. "I never understood the thing with the kids. I could put up with a lot of annoyances for three hundred million, couldn't you?"

"I expect," I had to agree. "What do you think is their problem?"

"I don't know. Stupidity? Unvarnished greed? Some kinds of financial pressures on them?"

"Any ideas of the pressures?"

"Not firsthand, no—"

"Secondhand?"

"Orville used to grouse about it. Francine was a drug addict, he said—only when you are that rich, there are nicer names for it. Drug dependent, whatever."

"She sick?"

"Oh, no, just likes the buzz, I guess. Brenda's the sick one. Depression. But she's the best of the lot. But then, her husband may be the worst."

"What's Lolly like?"

"Nice enough airhead. Defers to her husband—"

"And he?"

"On first meeting, he's aces. Personable, bright, engaging. If you don't have to do any business with him, he's okay. Probably great for a round of golf. But ethically, he's a cipher. A man you should not trust farther than you could throw him, with his pants full of lead."

"Most likely to succeed at bumping the old man off?"

He shook his head. "He could hire the hit man," he said. "But he'd stiff him on the compensation. Somehow—make a deal, then change it—don't pay the second installment." He shook his head again. "I don't see it. He'd be dead by this time, too."

"Hit by the hit man?"

"Exactly!"

"There were some calls to Mexico on the phone bill. Know anything about it?"

"Mexico?" He scrunched his upper lip. "He had a deal in Mexico some years ago, but it didn't go through. It was one of those fat farms—Orville was in his fat period—he was working his way up to sixty and eating a lot of rich foods—and I wouldn't be surprised if he were drinking a bit on top of it. That's the way he was—instead of just going to a fat farm, he tried to buy it. From a woman, as I recall. He had about talked her right into it, then poof—it went up in smoke."

"Any idea why?"

"No," he said, frowning. "That was somewhat unusual, though—him trying to buy something and failing."

"Didn't happen before?"

"Not in my experience."

"When was this…offer to purchase?"

"I don't remember—fifteen, twenty years ago."

"La Puerta del Sol was the place on the phone bill. Sound familiar?"

"Could be. I don't know—I never was much good at those Spanish names."

"There was also a medical clinic of some sort. I couldn't get much out of them. Know anything about that?"

"No. Orville was a bit of a hypochondriac," he said reluctantly, as though telling an unhappy tale out of school. "Always imagining he had this illness or that. He'd go anywhere at the slightest hint of a cure for his imaginary aches and pains."

"Sure they were all imaginary?"

He shrugged. "Who knows?"

"Do you think Orville expected to be killed?"

"Must have crossed his mind," he said with a peculiar lift of the corners of his mouth—an action that could have been construed as a smile—if I didn't know better.

"He ever talk to you about it?"

"Not really. Just that he was doing it. I think he feared his sons-in-law. A motley bunch, to my way of thinking. At the time, I thought it was paranoia—now, I'm not so sure."

"Could the wife have done it? Pamela?"

He seemed surprised. "I don't see how she could improve her lot by killing him."

"Kids say he was tiring of her and she feared she would be cut out of his will."

"Hmm." He shook his head. "How much less would she get in a divorce? Orville wasn't cheap with his ex-wives. They all got handsome settlements. No reason to think Pamela would have gotten anything less. She's had some longevity on the others."

"He take any action about reducing her inheritance?"

"Not that I know."

"Who did his will—"

"Lawyers—"

"Name?"

"Elsie Frankenhalter—" His eyelashes popped up again. I thought I'd wrung him dry. I took his facial response to mean there was something unusual about Elsie Frankenhalter, but he would only say, "See for yourself."

I called for an appointment. Her secretary told me Elsie was a very busy woman without a lot of time to fritter away on the likes of me. Oh, there may have been some attempt to high fructose corn syrup coat that, but it melted away in the translation.

Persistence paid and she agreed to sandwich me in between two clients I was given to understand, were, owing to the nature of the "billable hours" system, ever so much more important than I.

TEN

ELSIE FRANKENHALTER didn't keep me waiting, I'll say that for her. I'll also say I had no trouble seeing immediately why old Zach raised his eyebrows. Elsie Frankenhalter was, in the vernacular, a major babe. And there was no dumbing down clotheswise—no gray suit with a white blouse and even a possible ersatz necktie to help her blend in with the old boy network.

No, she wore rather sheer tights with a tannish hue, giving her the look of some well-toned and naked gams, a short skirt that made me nervous, and a pullover cashmere sweater that seemed tailor-made to accentuate the positive.

Her face was not one you'd picture glued to a law book. Indeed, being in her presence put your mind as far from the law as possible, and may even have nudged you with several laws you might want to break. She had fine, young lines, aristocratic cheek bones and lips stung by a wasp or other insect that would pump out more stuff than a bee. Her hair was curly and it fell all over the place.

She actually stood to greet me, giving me a very generous view of the real estate.

"What can I do for you, Mr. Yates?" she asked, letting me know there wasn't going to be time for chit chat.

I must have stared overlong because she said, "Is your question did Orville Sampson hire me for my looks?" She smiled like the Mona Lisa, which, as you know, is barely a smile. "Let's just say it didn't hurt."

There it was, no false modesty. I had to admit to myself, given the choice of Elsie Frankenhalter to represent me in the intimacies of the law, or some dried up old guy, it would be no contest. And no, I wouldn't care a persimmon for competence. I'd assume a law degree and the passing of the bar exam would guarantee minimum competence, as I'm sure Orville Sampson did.

I not only had a devil of a time formulating questions in Elsie's presence, I had some difficulty processing the answers.

I tried some questions that she had not already answered with her opening statement, but she waved them off. "Get to the point," she said. "Do I know why anyone would want to kill him? No. Did he express any fear of being murdered? I guess you'd have to say with that clause in his will, he had some thoughts, but he didn't share them with me."

That was a disappointment. I wanted to say something flip like, "What did he share with you?" but years of commerce at the feet of my father-in-law, the dandruff bag, taught me otherwise.

"No, we did not have an affair," she continued, unabashed. "I was in Sacramento the night he was killed, and no, if Orville was about to change his will, he had not told me about it. The last change was about six months before his death, where he added the codicil about not settling the estate in the event of suspected foul play, until any possible perpetrator was brought to justice and convicted."

I opened my mouth to speak. She didn't give me any opportunity.

"Yes, I know that could take years. Orville knew it, too. He laughed and said that he wouldn't be in any hurry after he was gone. The kids had filed suit to get control of the trusts out of his hands. You might imagine if you had put three hundred fifty million in trust for each of your kids, such bizarre ingratitude might smart a little. Of course, the trusts were for Orville's tax benefit—but the kids didn't seem to realize they were for their benefit as well. It stands to reason if he paid taxes on the money, the trusts would each be lighter by about one hundred fifty million. It gives an odd perspective to the childrens' complaints."

"Did…" I started; she answered the questions of her choosing.

"No, I don't know what he did with the substantial cash withdrawals the last six months of his life. He didn't give any of it to me. I'm told he had one or more girlfriends, but he never discussed that with me. I believe he gave them some of the cash, but a half million? I doubt it, though I do understand some women have a genius for extracting money from men. I, alas, was never one of them. I have a husband, who if he ever worked a day in his life, I wasn't around for it. Don't ask why I keep him. I haven't the faintest idea."

She looked me in the eye. "Will that about do it?"

"I…"

She looked at her watch. "You have time for one question," she said as though she were a press secretary at a president's press conference.

I had no time to think. "Did anyone ever tell you you had pretty blue eyes?" I blurted.

That maddening Mona Lisa smile returned to her wasp-stung lips. She stood to usher me to the door.

"They're green," she said, and before I even realized it, I was out the door.

So much for the irresistible charms of Gil Yates, private eye.

ELEVEN

I DON'T WANT TO SAY I had an easy time locating Brianna Lynn Tawney, the last known amour of the late great Orville Sampson. Suffice to say, I could write a book about the travails, none too interesting, leading up to the final pounce in her penthouse apartment on Wilshire Blvd., viewing distance to UCLA.

Orville had been circumspect. No checks, no notes—*nada*. Finally, with Pamela's reluctant permission ("Is it necessary to dredge all that up? The man is dead." "Yes, but you want to find out who killed him, so it *is* necessary.")

I can tell you, Orville Sampson made a *lot* of phone calls. After winnowing out the known numbers—home, office, business associates—he was a man who made a lot of his own calls—I was left with about a thousand others.

I clustered them to winnow out the calls made only a handful of times. My best shot was calls made to the same number numerous times. A handful of numbers popped out.

A lot of numbers were to homes of his business associates, lawyer, accountant and doctor. It was a tribute to the power of wealth, I thought, to have a doctor's home telephone number.

So *I* made a lot of phone calls, giving more or less the same pitch to each receptor: "Hello—I'm Gil Yates—doing an investigation for Pamela Sampson into her husband's death. Your name appears on his telephone bill, and I wonder if you could tell me anything about the conversations you had with him—anything that might shed light on his mysterious death." I didn't say murder—it was a turn off. I didn't want them to think they were suspect.

I'd become hardened to the worthless response— "Oh, he called me about…" and it would be some innocuous business detail from one of his many corporate raids—repeated conversations and coercions, the subjects of which all seemed nothing out of the ordinary, and no one—even those Orville Sampson bested in their financial world—expressed any animosity toward Sampson.

Nothing made much sense until I got an answer that, on the surface, made no sense whatsoever. After my spiel there was a three second lull. Then this honeybaked ham with a maple syrup voice opened fire.

"I know the man, I know him well—
That doesn't mean I care to tell

Any tall tales out of school.
I'm very private, as a rule.

But you sound mighty cute,
Kind of sensual to boot.
Perhaps we could meet
Somewhere on the street.

I could check you out,
See if Brianna still doubt
Your bona fide credentials.
I'll overlook a few essentials.

"Maybe you're the man
To whom I can
Tell my woeful tale
Without going to jail.

So, I'll see you at the corner at eight.
Promise me you won't be late.
I promise I won't give you the gate
If you show me some love and no hate."

"What corner, Brianna?"

"Come ahead,
I'll make my bed.

I'll tidy up
And give you a cup."

"Hey, hey, Brianna, why all this rap stuff?"

"I don't call it rap, my rhyme.
I'm not gonna be trapped any time.
One so garrulous, innocent and young
Must be careful of her tongue.

Besides, rhyme makes me think
So my brain doesn't go down the sink.
Moreover, it's not like greed and pestilence
This intriguing quality I call reticence."

"*Brianna!* The *corner?*"

"Just down the street
Is where we'll meet.
At Wilshire and Beverly Glen.
So, toodle oooo, till then."

She hung up. "At eight," she had said, but she didn't
say what night. Or did she mean the AM? I called her
back. After four rings, her answering machine clicked on.

"Sad to say Brianna is not here."
No need to shed a tear.

On this tape if you can yak,
The Queen of Angels will call you back."

I told Tyranny Rex I was working late, and headed for Wilshire and Beverly Glen.

Westwood, home of UCLA and smart people. Chic—slim, pretty, hustling. (The corner had one of those upscale pizza parlors that catered to the stars in the hopes of attracting the star struck.)

I didn't have the slightest trouble recognizing Brianna—knee high black leather boots, a black leather mini skirt, a clinging black turtleneck with a black leather vest that nicely framed two of nature's greatest achievements. Her hair was black, pulled straight back in a bun. Her skin was also black—not high yellow, mulatto, quadroon or a suntanned white—black black. She was the poster child for the "Black is Beautiful" campaign.

Her skin shone in the light of the street lamp, as though she were swimming in champagne, and I'm not sure she wasn't.

I found myself tongue-tied in her presence—like I should be speaking in verse, though I can't imagine anything worse.

Brianna didn't wait to turn on her hip hop.

"Well, hell-ooo there, Mr. Dick—
You could make a girl mighty love sick.

Um, um, you are one slick puppy.
I can tell you are one big man—no guppy.

"I expect you'll be wanting to buy me a drink.
We'll talk, and if we make the link,
Maybe we'll go back to my place,
And I'll invite you into my private space."

"How did you meet Orville Sampson, Brianna?"

"We had a drink in a bar,
Soon I was in the back seat of a car.
That caddy wasn't moving,
We were more or less grooving.

"We wasted no time on cat and mouse.
Before you knew it, I had my penthouse.
And me, a poor girl from the hood.
I didn't beg—he thought that was good."

"How do you account for your sudden success?"

"There are certain aspects
Of me, as you might expects,
The big man did not find
Unappealing to his fussy mind."

She twirled around like a model and I could see
what she meant. She steered me into the pizza place

that was blessed with a full bar. I had designer water,
she went stronger. Some sissy drink with pineapple
slices and a tiny umbrella.

Brianna had a genius for picking up where she left off:

"So I hop on down to the high fashion store,
And buy me an outfit that costs no more
Than a Cadillac car or Mercedes bus,
And, oo, oo, oo, Ollie made such a fuss.

"You should have seen me in those threads.
I was dashing, as a woman of a hundred beds.
My cheek Ollie gave a mighty tweak,
And said, 'My dear, you're awfully chic.'"

"Brianna, this is enormous fun, but what can you
tell me about his family, for instance?"

"Oooeee, those girls, they're spoiled rotten.
Bodies misshapen, and minds misbegotten.
They never work, they got too much;
With common folk they're out of touch."

"It seems they married fairly common husbands,"
I said.

"Those nutso sons-in-laws
Are nothing but teeth and claws.

They don't stand too tall,
Still, I'd keep my back to the wall."

"So you met Orville's daughters and their husbands?"

"No, no, Brianna don't have to meet.
He tells me all, my Ollie, my sweet.
And in his confidence the big man takes me,
Now we're soulmates for all eternity."

Just when I despaired of getting anything useful
from Brianna, she came out with this:

"My man, he tells me things.
When we love, he's like a bird who sings.
Two kids sued, and one did not.
But, verily, he's the worst of the lot.

"Now, I won't tell you what to do,
But if little me were, like, little you,
I'd spend my time on that pipsqueak snot.
That's when you'll find out what's what."

TWELVE

I THOUGHT I WAS SO CLEVER enlisting Pamela Sampson's help in drawing the pipsqueak snot, Kurt Roberts, away from his homestead so I could question his beleaguered wife, Lolly. It was, after all, she who put the bird in my ear, so to speak, about her hubby's liaison with the inimitable Pamela (there is no secret, only enthusiasm) Sampson.

In retrospect, I realize I put poor Lolly at a disadvantage, not making an appointment or giving her any warning that I might be coming. She'd seemed so helpless and innocent, I didn't see how it could matter.

Lolly greeted me at the door as though I were an apparition. She was dressed in a skimpy skirt of a reddish hue, that, on closer inspection, turned out to be leather. She wore no shoes or socks. Her halter top was white spandex, which did a more or less imperfect job of keeping those nicely developed glands in check.

She was obviously dressed for something and it wasn't housework.

My first thought was that Pamela Sampson had spilled the string beans about my surprising Lolly, and she was going to make a shameful play for me.

Alas, that was not to be. Instead, Lolly looked flustered, frazzled and frustrated. Like I was the last person she wanted to see.

"Oh…Mr…?"

"Yates," I said.

"Yes—sorry, this is not a good time," she said, shooting me a look that telegraphed a certain urgency. "My husband doesn't want me to talk to you if he's not here."

"He's not here?" I faked it.

"No—not just now."

"Expect him back soon?"

"No. I—"

"I could wait," I offered.

"Oh, no, that wouldn't be—"

"Look, Lolly, we all want to solve this thing, I'm trying, but I need your help. You told me about Kurt and Pamela—you think that's where he is now?"

"I don't—he doesn't tell me where he goes…"

With a sudden spurt of *chutzpah* I bolted into the room and made myself comfy on the couch. Lolly looked startled.

"What can you tell me about Kurt and Pamela? You hinted at something when I was here before."

"Really," she said. "You have to go—"

"Well, not really," I said. "If Kurt isn't coming back soon, we have some time."

Her eyes bulged. She was thinking feverishly and

the thoughts weren't pleasant. Her eyes never left the front window and the expanse of the driveway beyond.

"Tell me about the dogs," I said, as they began to yip in the backyard.

"I hate them!" She spat the words out impulsively.

"Why do you have them?"

"We? *He!* That's Kurt's thing. I swear he's training them to take my leg off. If I go out back when Kurt's out there, the dogs lunge at me and sniff my crotch. Kurt thinks that is enormously funny."

"Is Kurt having an affair with Pamela Sampson?"

She frowned. "My sisters tell me he is."

"Sour grapes?"

She looked out the window, her body rigid with an unstated fear. "I'm not talking about my husband. If you get it wrong, and he's implicated, I could lose my share."

"Oh, I don't think…you know, if the police haven't nailed one of you, there mustn't be anything to worry about." I watched her face—she wanted to believe.

"Why didn't he join the suit after he convinced the others to sue?" I asked as though she hadn't protested—and she answered!

"Kurt thought if a settlement was offered, he could decide if he wanted to accept, depending how much it was. He could always hold out for the whole enchilada when Orville died."

"Was he sick?"

"Well, he was seventy-six years old and he always was

a hypochondriac. He had pills to go to bed by, pills to get up by, pills to eat by, pills to go to the bathroom by."

"Ever hear of a woman named Brianna Tawney?"

She frowned. "I don't think so."

"Know what your father could have done in Mexico?"

She kept her eyes on the window.

"Lolly," I said, "why are you looking out the window all the time?"

She jerked her head away from the glass. "I'm not," she said.

"If Kurt comes home, just tell him you didn't know I was coming, and told me you couldn't answer any questions, and I'll ask them all over, carefully selected, of course."

That didn't seem to put her at ease.

"Mexico?" I prodded. "Mean anything?"

"Oh, I don't know. Maybe he had some business there once upon a time. He was always buying things."

"Anything recently?"

"Not that I know of."

Lolly's body suddenly had a spasm so pronounced, I feared she was having an epileptic fit. Her eyes were out the window and her body seemed to follow. "Excuse me," she said rapidly, "I've got to go out a minute." And she was out the door and down the steps in record time.

Not being one especially adept at minding my own business, I stood to get a better vantage point to peer out the big window in front.

Lolly was leaning over the driver's window, engaged in earnest conversation with the lone occupant of a rather modest, well-used car. He was one of those well-scrubbed teenagers that every mother wants: handsome, mannerly and…young.

Lolly raised up and stood back as the lad turned the car around and drove down the driveway, craning his neck to watch Lolly in the rearview mirror.

For her part, Lolly ran her palms down the side of her skirt to make sure, I suppose, that it hadn't jumped up while she was conversing with the lad. She turned, almost militarily, and marched back up the porch, doing her darnedest to do her duty.

I greeted her, still standing. "I'm sorry," I said. "I didn't realize you were expecting a visitor."

"I wasn't," she snapped, a lady protesting too much. "He's just…a friend."

I nodded sympathetically. "Well, I'll be going. I hope it's not too late—I mean, I didn't ruin it, did I?"

"There's nothing to ruin. He's just a…friend. Not even a friend, really—an acquaintance."

I nodded again, even more sympathetically.

"He's one of those Mormon proselytizers," she said, explaining more than she had to. "He comes by every so often, and if I'm alone, I pass the time listening to his spiel. It fills my loneliness sometimes."

I'll bet it does, I thought. "Thinking of becoming a Mormon?" I asked, and I was ashamed of myself for it.

"Oh, no," she answered quickly. "It's just—as I say—a pastime."

"Yeah, well, good," I said. "It's nice to have friends."

"Yeah," she said.

"Well, I'll be on my way," I said.

I didn't have far to go—around the block, actually— when I saw the lad's car parked behind the house. I sped by it, checking my rearview.

Handsome opened his car door, alighted and made his way to the servant's entrance.

I parked the car and made my way to the front and the convenient cover of some bushes. The dogs, thank goodness, were cooped up in back. I found it fascinating the dogs kept their peace while Mr. Mormon transgressed their territory. He must have done a lot of proselytizing.

I lay in wait with a decent view of the living room window. I didn't have long to wait. It was my good fortune that the urgency was such they didn't have time to close the drapes.

Lolly's skirt soon became even more mini—the halter failed to halt what it was meant to halt and the dislocations of the body coverings revealed a lot of gorgeous real estate.

They seemed to be very close friends, indeed. It was enough to turn the hardest heart to Mormonism.

THIRTEEN

MEXICO. THERE HAD been a couple of phone calls to Mexico—two numbers—one was a fat farm, another a medical clinic. Neither place acknowledged knowing Orville Sampson. Both places were large with many employees, and no one seemed willing to amass them all to see who Orville called.

I didn't see how I could put off going to Mexico—nor did I see how I could blindside Tyranny Rex and sneak out for the requisite time to investigate.

I called the fat farm and asked for a brochure, and immediately realized the call would be on my phone record, should anyone care to check.

When it came, I carefully left it lying carelessly in the living room, in close proximity to some of Tyranny's darling glass figurines—which was no trick because everywhere in the living room was in close proximity to Tyranny's figurines.

I started peppering my conversation with the handful of Spanish words I had mastered in service of several of our apartment gardeners. *¿Cómo está?* (How are you?) *Hasta luego* (until later) *¿Qué Pasa?* (What's happening?) As you can see, my Spanish was more or less dazzling.

"*¿Qué pasa, mi esposa?*" I asked my spouse (what's happening, my wife?). She looked at me with a countenance of disdain. She was not sufficiently erudite to appreciate my command of the Spanish language. She didn't know one word, and was eaten alive with envy.

I always felt my lack of appreciation for Dorcas's glass figurines bespoke a parallel lack of artistic taste.

Tyranny, had, to put it bluntly, filled out a bit since my last case, *Ship Shapely*. She always had prodigious lungs, but now the rest of her was catching up with a vengeance.

I expected Tyranny would ask me about it, to which inquiry a response would be fielded on the order of ultimate casualness: "Oh, I thought I might try it sometime." Her response was sure to be, "Have a good time, I'll be tied up with a show (of her darling glass figurines)."

And that was where I made my mistake—in thinking La Puerta del Sol in old Mexico was the last place Tyranny Rex would want to go.

So, a few nights later at dinner (she made her signature dish—macaroni and cheese—from a box), I casually mentioned I might take in a few days at this health spa in old Mexico (there is no *new* Mexico in old Mexico).

She looked at me as though I had lost my little round things—but that wasn't that different from how she usually looked at me. So naturally, I thought, I *hoped,* the first words out of her mouth would be, "You're crazy!" Instead, she said, "What a *wonder*ful idea. I'll go with you."

"Oh," I said, swallowing, "oh, I thought you had a show."

"Only this weekend."

"That's when I was going," I quickly added, "for a whole week."

She gave me one of her looks that made me cry within for more domestic backbone. "What's your hurry?"

"Oh, no hurry," I said. "I just felt like it."

"Well, feel like it next week."

I pursed my lips pusillanimously, then shook my head. "*You* can go next week, I've got some surveys to do for your father. I think I'll go this week."

There was that look again, frozen in time for just an instant that seemed like forever. She put both hands on the edge of the table, as though preparatory to launching herself to the moon. (I should *be* so lucky.) "All right," she said, "this week, then."

"Oh, but I don't want you to miss your show."

She waved a hand of dismissal. "Oh, it's only a local show. This will be good for me. I've been notic-ing I've been putting on a few pounds—"

I almost sprayed a mouthful of macaroni and cheese her way. A *few*, I thought.

But the eye was cast, or the die was rolled, or something like that.

Being alone in a car with Tyranny Rex for a long trip was not what I'd call unmitigated joy. I can't remember how long it has been since I've been suckered into that particular torture chamber. She usually says something outrageous, and it is all I can do to keep from poking her one.

Of course, heretofore, that is, before I backed into this private eye game, I was afraid to say "boo" to Dorcas, or her fatuous father, Daddy Dandruff. My livelihood depended on their goodwill. Thus, I had this funny notion that the way to their goodwill was to be pusillanimous and mealy mouthed, which, happily or un-, became second nature to me.

But now that I have been successful at this shamus sport, when I could tell both Tyranny and Daddybucks to take a flying leap off Mount Rushmore, I find myself quaintly reticent—who was it said, "You have a lot of trouble teaching a cool cat new tricks?" It could be a genetic failing, for God knows mankind would be immeasurably improved with Tyranny Rex and Daddybucks spread-eagled, face down at the base of Mount Rushmore.

So we were driving along the next day, below San Juan Capistrano someplace, I was minding my own business, and Tyranny seemed congenitally unable to do the same. "Malvin," she began, and whenever she used my name, I was primed to expect trouble. Like Pavlov's dog.

"Did you ever think, when we got married, that twenty-five years later, you'd still be working for Daddy Wemple?"

The question stunned me. The embarrassing thing was, I didn't think about it at all. I was conditioned to believe that I had made the most salubrious catch in all the world, and I was damn lucky to take anything that was doled out to me. How was a guy like me going to make a living, anyway?

Of course, when Tyranny asked me a question, I learned over the years, she wasn't so much interested in my answer as she was in giving me *her* opinion on the subject. I played my part in the scene. "I didn't think about it much, I guess," I said. "What did you think?"

"Oh," she said, trying to fake casual, "I had this wish that you'd crawl out from under Daddy Wemple's influence and go out on your own once you learned the business—start your own company—give him a run for his money."

That was a startling revelation, indeed, that Dorcas would even entertain the notion that her milquetoast husband would deign to compete with that great god, her gasbag father, Elbert August Wemple, Realtor Ass.

"You ever hear of this guy, Sampson?" I asked to

pass the time. "The one with the three daughters—put a lot of money in trust—"

"I read about that," she said. "Weren't they suing him, or something?"

"Two of them were," I said.

"What about it?" she said with that charging edge she sharpens her speech with. It's enough to make Superman back off. I did some footwork.

"I was just thinking, he had all that money, and look what happened."

"What happened?"

"Well, he puts three hundred million or so in trust for each of them, and two of them aren't satisfied, so they sue him."

"Sue him for what?"

"To get control of the dough. They apparently don't like how he is spending some of the interest."

"I don't follow your reasoning. Why do you bring this up?"

"Oh, well, I was just thinking, in the context of your disappointment in me not going out and getting as rich as Daddybucks."

"Daddy Wemple," she corrected me. "Let's not be disrespectful."

"Well, somebody killed him, apparently—"

"Daddy Wemple?"

"No, Sampson. Do you think one of his kids could have had it done? There was a lot of money involved."

"You never know nowadays."

We drove in silence, which was my preferred mode of travel with Tyranny Rex.

"Do you think one of our kids could kill a parent?"

She frowned for only a moment. "You, maybe," she said.

FOURTEEN

NEW WORLD, old world, third world and Mexico. Crossing the border to Tecate, Mexico, was like entering the fourth world. Unencumbered by any architectural restraints, the town seemed to lend itself to impoverished gunslingers restoring honor to some dishonored señorita.

It was a sunny place, and Confucius say, "The more sun, the less gumption."

Crossing the boundary of the property owned and operated by La Puerta del Sol deposited us suddenly smack back in world *numero uno*. The structures were American versions of Mexican chic. Lots of good old expensive red tile roofs, immaculate pathways of adobe tiles. Neat and clean trees, shrubbery and flowers galore, highlighting the lush lawns.

The grass looked like it had been laid by a hoity-toity wall-to-wall carpet emporium with seamless perfection.

Maybe that was where Orville Sampson had picked up his fondness for grass.

Tyranny and I settled in a cutsie stucco cottage decorated in Beverly Hills Southwest, complete with the pregnant stucco fireplace in the corner that cried out for a loaf of warm bread and those colorful Mexican throw rugs.

The first thing that struck me about La Puerta del Sol was there didn't seem to be any fat people there. It was a fat farm for those already obsessive about their weight and had done a good job of knocking off any fat that might have encroached on their bones. But the people creeping around the neat-as-a-needle grounds looked like the "after" shots in those gym ads.

The dining hall was a two story brown adobe brick—the upstairs was used for those diners who took a vow of silence at mealtime—and if you listened to the tenor of the conversation downstairs you'd see just how astute that was.

Off to the corner out front were a cluster of a half dozen huge *Washingtonia* palm trees with the dead fronds swaying like modest hula skirts over the stiff trunks. Not far off was a giant pepper tree—half a block in diameter. The grounds were planted in an assortment of drought-tolerant stuff like Yuccas and Prickly Pear Cactus. A couple of pink Ablaze trees framed the entry. Low prolific flowers and some yellow-green Junipers rounded out the set.

As soon as we hit the dining hall for our first dinner, I could see why there were no fat people here. The fare wasn't low fat, it was fat free. Our salad was lettuce with lemon juice, the entrée a nice tofu enchilada.

I came to look upon these meals as fasting. While I was at La Puerta del Sol, I never got hungry. It was the only place I knew of where you could spend all your time eating and still lose weight. No fat, no sugar; a lot of fiber.

I was looking forward to the beginning of the exercise classes when Tyranny would be distracted, so I could make my inquiries.

I actually considered coming sanitized with Tyranny about my mission here, but then I realized she would probably laugh her head off at the improbability of it all.

Starting the next morning, my Tyranny was like a pig in barley waddling between absolutely abs—where the focus was on abdominal muscles that Tyranny hadn't seen in a couple of decades—and step aerobics, where, if I knew anything, Tyranny had to be hoisted on and off the step with a forklift.

She also favored the water exercises where her superior buoyancy made lifting her fire hydrant thighs somewhat easier.

Myself, I eschewed this strenuous life and, while I told Tyranny I was going to some competing maniacal exercise session, I sought the boss of the farm.

I used my impeccable Spanish on select members of the staff and found my way up a brick tree-lined path to a modest cottage off the dining room.

It was about half the size of our suite, and when I

knocked gently on the door (no intimidation from me), a rather strong, but feminine, voice sounded a come in bell, and I did.

She was seated at a fairly cluttered desk and she exhibited exemplary posture. Her straight gray hair was pulled back in a pony tail. She smiled at me as I introduced myself and she told me her name.

Vivian Moloski must have broken a potload of hearts in her career. I could picture that straight gray hair a saucy, flouncy blond, her purple eyes locked in love with those of the right swain who came down the pike with his fellows who were, in her estimation, just as right. There was enough gleam in those purple orbs to disarm a tank battalion.

She waved me to a chair before I stated my business.

"I'm investigating the murder of a man who called here before he died. Orville Sampson—"

She almost fell out of her chair. "So, someone finally got him," she said. "I'd look for a woman."

"Oh." I cocked an eyebrow—the left, as I remember. "How so?"

She shook her head, seemingly transported back in time to a pleasant, but aggravating memory.

"We'd had some correspondence—he'd heard I was vulnerable to an offer to purchase. My husband of twenty-seven years had just run off with a teenager to find himself in the mountains, somewhere south of here."

"Did he find himself?"

"I don't know. I never found him. Anyway, I was beside myself. He'd started the place and I hadn't the least notion I could handle the operation. Enter the white knight, Mr. Orville Sampson. Well, he swept me right off my feet, he was so charming. Not that I wasn't vulnerable. But, did you say he called before he died? How long before?"

"Several times in the six months before."

She shook her head. "He didn't call me," she said. "He knew better."

There was some bitterness there. I gave her a moment to explain. She didn't. I didn't press.

"Who did he call," I asked, "any idea?"

She shook her head resolutely. Then a frown took over her forehead. "I wonder," she muttered, then abandoned the idea.

"Wondered what?" I prodded.

"Oh, nothing."

"Is there any way we could find out who he talked to?"

She was frowning still—lost in thought. "If you will excuse me," she said, in a fog, "I'm not myself. This is a shock and a memory I don't wish to relive."

It seemed to me a delicate line—did I press her to aggravate her—or back off to return another day?

"I'll be here a week," I said. "May we talk later?"

"I don't know," she said. "See if I can get over the shock—"

"Is there anyone I could talk to who might know who he called here?"

"No, no," she said, waving that hand to signal her fervent wish for my departure.

I departed.

I left the cottage/office abruptly enough to catch a middle aged maid in the act of eavesdropping. She turned abruptly from me and hurried down the path toward the back of the dining building. I followed.

"Hey!" I said, but she walked faster. I ran after her and, owing only to her hefty size, I was able to catch up.

"What were you doing outside Vivian's office?" I demanded when I had blocked her path.

"*No comprendo,*" she said, but I figured she comprendoed all right, or she wouldn't be listening at the window of her boss's office.

At any rate, I tried some of my dazzling Spanish on her and she didn't *comprendo* that, either.

She dodged me with the grace of a trapped cat and ducked into the kitchen via the back door.

Easy come, easy lose.

FIFTEEN

THERE WEREN'T ANY TELEPHONES in the rooms at La Puerta del Sol, in an effort, I suppose, to keep the blood pressure down. Mexico, I discovered, had a more civilized ratio of phones to people than El Norte. My Tyranny Rex had more phones herself than a lot of Mexican villages.

La Puerta del Sol did have a telephone in the cottage that passed for a main desk—every establishment needed a place to pay your bills.

I sauntered in, as casually as I could, to ask my question of a pretty young woman at the desk. She had radiant black hair that bounced off her shoulders and a constitution that could operate independent of my goodwill.

She brought her head up from her desk, but not her concentration. "Yes," she said.

"I'm a guest here," I said, putting on a broad, friendly smile. I almost used my pseudonym, Gil Yates. "Stark's the name," I mumbled. She didn't care. "A friend of mine was murdered," I said, and paused to see if she was still breathing.

I think she was, for she said, "Not here—?"

"No, but he made some calls to this number before he was killed. You know how I could find out who he might have talked to?"

"We don't keep records of incoming calls."

"But I notice you don't keep phones in your rooms."

"No."

"So he would have had to call someone on the staff?"

"We will take messages for guests."

"Do you call them to the phone?"

"Not usually. The cottages are spread all over the place—there are many activities going on—we don't know where people are most of the time."

"Do you write messages and deliver them to the room?"

"Yes."

"Do you keep a record of the messages?"

"No...I told you..." Patience was not her long apparel.

"How long have you been answering the phone here?"

"Over two years. But I only answer in the daytime."

"Who does it the other times?"

"Different people. It's not a regular thing, night duty—could be almost anybody."

I knew from Orville's phone records most of the calls were made in the afternoon, but there could have been shift crossovers.

"The name Orville Sampson ring a bell with you?"

She frowned. "No," she said. "I get so many calls, I don't retain any names."

"Well, if you think of anything that will help—" Then I had visions of her spilling the beans to Tyranny and I hastily added, "I'll stop back before I leave."

I thanked her, for what I don't know, and when I stepped out of the cottage, the same uniformed woman was scurrying down the path.

I once again gave chase, until she ducked into a ladies bathroom, where I waited for her to come out, only to see Tyranny Rex scurrying herself, as far as that were possible, with a towel, robe and bathing cap, heading for one of those swimming pool buoyant pastimes. I abandoned my stake out and did the sociable thing—accompanied her to the large pool where she was to engage in her next workout session.

Myself, I was dressed in shorts and a T shirt that held the wisdom:

If a man speaks
in a forest and
there is no woman
to hear him, is he
still wrong?

The idea was to throw Tyranny Rex off the scent. Make her think I was hopping from class to class, as she was.

She went to beginning aerobics, I said I was trying intermediate. I actually went to a class and found myself enamored of some kind of aerobic dance where we took three steps obliquely to the left and clapped twice beside the left temple, and three oblique steps to the right and clapped once beside the right temple. Adorable! I quickly developed a case on the instructor—a young, pleasantly shaped woman with a deformed arm and an infectious, bubbly enthusiasm. Lucy her name was.

I watched Tyranny lower herself into the pool and was pleasantly surprised that no tidal wave engulfed those of us left on shore.

I watched her a respectable amount of time as she clung to the wall and lifted first one leg, then the other—until I was absolutely certain she forgot I was there (about eight seconds).

I filled the rest of the daylight hours analyzing who might have answered Orville Sampson's calls. I mentally broke the possibilities down to staff, teachers and guests. The staff consisted, I thought, of the kitchen staff, grounds staff, maids and desk and administration. I would try to ask a few of each if they knew anything about Orville Sampson or anyone who knew him, but I decided Orville Sampson's real interest would be the exercise people who were in the peak of condition. For verily, it was said Orville Sampson had an eye for the female flesh.

A cute waitress was another possibility, as was a staff member—perhaps even the filly who answered the phone.

Luckily, a guest was more remote, since the calls were spread over five weeks and guests generally stay for one or two weeks.

The telephone people would have heard the name if they were writing notes to the guests. So, unless there was a concerted cover up, the toughest category could be overlooked.

I decided one of those well-built instructors might be the most fertile ground, but there was a hitch. The exercise staff changed—rotated. One couldn't stay in this isolated Mexican hamlet indefinitely—and nice as the fat farm was, going stir crazy was an occupational hazard.

That afternoon, while Tyranny was having her burgeoning flesh pounded, massaged and manipulated, I made some inquiries.

A sullen gardener didn't seem to connect with what I was saying in English or Spanish.

The maids I encountered were shy, and the name Orville Sampson seemed to mean nothing to them. I was wondering if soon I would decide Orville Sampson had never called here, and the whole thing was a big mix-up and I had wasted the trip—except for the maid, or kitchen helper, who always seemed to be listening when I was talking to anyone.

Before dinner, I caught my aerobic instructor after one of her classes. She was coming out of the room where a number of the faithful had been jiggling the flesh.

"There's my aerobic animal!" Lucy greeted me so effusively, I had to remind myself here I was Malvin Stark, not Gil Yates.

"Hi, Lucy," I said. "Have a good day?"

"Oh, yes!" she enthused. "Fantastic!"

"Lucy—you don't happen to know a man named Orville Sampson, do you?"

"Well, yes, I do, too," she said with a happy smile. Her memory of him seemed more pleasant than Vivian Moloski's.

"How?"

"Well, he spent a few days here a few months ago. Came to my classes. A real classy guy."

"You get to know him at all?"

"Not much, no. I just know he was beaucoup rich, and he wasn't affected at all by his money. He was just as nice as could be."

"But at the cost of this place, I don't suppose you get too many poor people, do you?"

"Well, no, but Sampson was mega-rich."

"Any suspicions on who killed him or might have wanted to?"

"Gosh, no. He wasn't killed here, was he?"

"No," I said. "You haven't heard anyone talking about it?"

"No. Who would know him?"

"Well, apparently, you did."

"Not really. He came to a couple of classes."

"Why would he?"

"I don't know. To feel better—get in shape."

"What kind of shape was he in?"

"Pretty good, for his age. Was in his seventies, wasn't he?"

"Yeah. Can you remember anything strange about him—or anything in connection with him?"

She thought a moment. "No. What kind of thing? He was just a normal attendee here."

"Seem happy?"

"Yeah, did to me."

I wasn't getting anywhere. I changed the subject. "By the way, can you tell me what happened to your arm—is that a birth thing?"

"No, my ex shot me," she said as though she were telling me what time it was.

"Oh, Lord," I said. "Where'd that happen?"

"L.A.," she said. "He had a lot of anger."

That was a contender for the understatement of the year prize.

"Is he in jail?"

"Oh, no. He had money and connections. They didn't even take his guns from him."

"Can't you do anything about it?"

"I went on a crusade for a while, but…it was all so

hopeless. When you are against money and power—"
She shrugged.

"His family was rich?"

"Not directly—no—but…he had contacts."

I was getting more curious just as she said she had to be off to an instructors' meeting. We made a date for the following afternoon when she promised to tell all.

Dinner that evening was par for the courses. Lettuce with vinegar, whole wheat pasta with boiled tomatoes. I'd rather not mention the dessert, which from time immemorial has been constructed of nourishing sugars and fats, but in the hands of these demoniacal chefs, is made of something else entirely. I suppose a book could be written on the culinary uses and abuses of styrofoam, but perhaps another time.

After dinner, an old Woody Allen movie was offered to the unsuspecting, whose number I was not at this juncture, among.

I moseyed around the grounds, checking out the books in the library. Our room was a far piece from the center of things, and once you were in your digs, you were committed.

The library was nice, but sparse—I had read everything I wanted to, so I opted for the peace and tranquility of the cottage at the far end of the campus.

It was dark, and pine-needle-drop quiet, as I made my way on the series of paths that led to our cottage, which was called Sunflower. The cottages were named for birds and flowers and trees, depending on which neck of the woods it was in.

My mind was on the case and trying to find a key to unlocking the mystery of the phone calls to the fat farm. I had just been marveling how quiet the grounds were—there weren't even any TVs in the rooms, and the cottages were isolated from the main paths, which got narrower the farther you got from the business end of the operation—when I heard a rustling in the bushes, so light I thought it was some nocturnal animal—perhaps a raccoon—and that's all I remember. Oh, I imagine, in moments of fantasy, that I heard the *thwack* of the blunt instrument to my head, but I'm not sure I did.

SIXTEEN

MY NEXT MEMORY—apart from the real or imagined thwacking sound to my head—was the menacing bulk of Tyranny Rex Stark looming large above me.

"Stay awake, Malvin. You could have a concussion and the doctor said you had to stay awake—so *stay awake!*"

She was fit to be chained. She was carrying on so, you'd think she had been the victim of the assault.

I quickly closed my eyes on the scene. The pain in my head was so excruciating, I didn't want to add that apparition of my beloved Tyranny to the agony. There is a cliché that explains it nicely, but I don't do clichés—gilding the liverwurst, or something.

With my eyes gently closed against the aggravation of Tyranny and the light, I had a sudden, silly notion that Tyranny Rex was responsible for my predicament. Somehow, I had been moved to the establishment's infirmary, where I imagined convicted bulimics were sent.

"Malvin!" her majesty's voice was commanding, accompanied by a slap to the cheeks, which could have been more gentle. "Who did this to you?"

That was Tyranny. As though being knocked unconscious had no bearing on getting the name, address and phone number of my assailant.

"Don't fall asleep," she commanded.

I grunted to let her know I was awake, though I'd rather not open my eyes just yet.

"Well!" Tyranny said with a *harumph,* as only she can, "I asked to see the person in charge, and they said that wouldn't be possible. 'Well!' I said, 'You'd better get him here right this minute or you're going to be one sorry puppy. The idea your grounds are unsafe from hoodlums, why, if word got out, it would close this place in minutes and you'd *all* be out of jobs.'

"Well! *She* came here on the double, I daresay, and she, I'm bound to tell you, is certifiably crackers. Do you know what she said? She said you were here investigating a murder! Can you just imagine? I've never heard anything so patently ridiculous in all my life! You! A detective! Oh my gawd. The woman is completely off her trolley, and I told her so in no uncertain terms. Imagine! Blaming you for snooping around and bringing this on yourself. And she didn't seem particularly put out that this had happened to you. Why, I've half a mind to pack up and get out of here."

That sentiment jolted me. No way could I walk out on this now. Oh, perhaps I'd have to shift my *modus operandi* ever so slightly; things like not walking alone at night. But one thing was certain, someone around here didn't want me around here.

Tyranny did her job keeping me awake—I won't say with a relish—as she slapped me into consciousness. The only thing she couldn't do was alleviate the pain.

In odd moments, when I could clear my head, I tried to analyze what had happened and how best to use the five days left to me here.

I knew one thing. I had to find out who was stalking me and why. And who was that eavesdropping maid?

The majoress domo had to tell me the rest of her story, too. But I couldn't hazard a guess on when I would be able to walk again without my head splitting open like an overripe watermelon.

Tyranny kept me awake all night. Keeping me alive must have caused internal conflict in my *esposa*. But she succeeded—and I don't doubt got something to talk about for twenty years.

Tyranny was raising holy hades with the staff, demanding a twenty-four hour guard on my person, and such was the force of her persuasiveness, they capitulated.

The gent they assigned to the day shift was a ninety-pound weakling, and I felt more secure with Tyranny at night. At least she had some heft on a would-be assailant.

It was a day and a half before I could get back to our cottage, and another day before I felt steady enough to ignore the pain and schlepp back to Vivian to finish her story, and perhaps shed some light on my mishap.

Vivian greeted me in her office with a sorry and solicitous face, but her true opinion was embodied in her words, "I just can't understand it, this has *never* happened here before." Translation: you must have brought it on yourself.

"Well, it wasn't self-inflicted, I can assure you," I said. "I'm not that strong."

"We are all sorry," Vivian said with a long face to prove it. "If there is anything else we can do…"

"There is," I cut in. "Finish your story about Orville Sampson. What made you change your mind about selling to him?"

She looked over my head. The memory was not a welcome visitor. "I think I told you my husband left me for a teenager—"

"Yes. To the mountains, to find himself, you said."

"Yes, well, that's my view of it, of course. His might be different."

"If I could find him—"

"Yes, of course," she said, as though she were reluctantly conceding a telling point.

"Soon thereafter, this man, Orville Sampson," I prodded her, "comes down and tries to buy the place—"

"*Too* soon," she said. "I was extremely vulnerable. I thought myself in love at first sight with that handsome Texan. Tall, virile, no fat on him, down-to-earth, friendly. He was just so…engaging."

"How long was he here?"

"Not long. Less than two weeks. But it was an intense time—we packed months into those twelve days. In retrospect, I acted too soon and too quickly—but I was frankly swept off my feet. All the while, a little voice was telling me he was using my emotions in service of his business interests, but what could I do? A helpless, middle-aged woman just cast on the manure pile of rejected women, when along comes this multimillionaire savior who pays me passionate court. I swear, the way I felt, I'd have *given* him the property—only…"

"Only?"

She looked over my head again. "I'm afraid, Mr. Stark, I really don't want to dredge up the gory details—it's too painful—"

"Painful?" I said, working up an outrage I seldom felt as Malvin Stark—I was being Gil Yates in a Malvin Stark persona. "I know something about painful, thanks to the little bop on the head I got on your premises. If I know anything about tort law, and I took it in my bashed head to be nasty, *I* might wind up owning your place."

She glared at me. I glared back. "Your blackmail, Mr. Stark, is not at all subtle."

"Thank you," I said. The glaring continued until

she broke her concentration and looked away. "In a way," she sighed, "I should be laughing. It happened so long ago. But…"

"He jilted you, didn't he?" I asked. "After a torrid romance?"

She stared at me just a moment, but it was an intimidating stare. I could see how this woman, heretofore so vulnerable, found strength to run this huge operation so successfully.

Then something loosened her.

"Torrid was it. That's the word. I'd never experienced anything like it. It began suddenly—with a head of steam—then ended just as suddenly."

"Why?" I asked.

"I wasn't enough for him." She shuddered—the nineteen-year-old memory still depressed her. "He… found…someone else." I thought "found" was an innocuous word in the context.

"Here?"

She nodded, then shook her head. "I was stupid, I guess. I thought he only had eyes for me. I was in my forties—cast off by a husband who apparently wanted to start over, and Orville was in his mid-fifties—old enough to settle down—not that I pushed marriage, or anything. It was too soon for that," she said, but I could tell it had more than crossed her mind.

"But who? Who did he find—some guest?"

She shook her head. "No, that might have been

more palatable. No, my Orville, prince among zillion-aires, found himself a pretty little señorita."

"In town? Or…here?"

"Oh, here, of course. A maid. She wasn't even his regular—she was a substitute. Don't ask me how it happened. It was a fluke I heard about it—back-door gossip—and when I confronted him, he didn't deny it. Had the audacity to think I would understand. 'She was so pretty,' he said, 'so innocent.'

"Well, you can imagine how that hit me like a ton of bricks—first my husband runs off with a teenager, then my lover does the same. I was a basketcase for months—it's like I was getting over one deadly illness only to be hit with another."

"What did you do?"

"As soon as I found out, I banished him from the property, of course." She frowned, as though search-ing for some memory she wasn't sure she wanted to find. "There was no question of my selling to him after that."

"Did he leave without any fuss?"

"Oh, yes. There was no misinterpreting my feelings. He couldn't stay a day longer."

"That was the end of the fling with the maid, too?"

"Well, I daresay. She lived in town in a hovel with her mother and father and a bushelful of siblings, and I couldn't see Orville Sampson, whatever his back-ground in dusty, dirt-floor Texas, moving in there. He couldn't stay here—it was a thoughtless one-night stand, anyway. Men!"

"And you haven't seen or heard from him since?"

"No! I put that two-timing monkey behind me and swore off men for the duration." She looked at her watch. "I have a meeting in five minutes," she said. "That's all I have time for." She stood. "I hope you're feeling better—say, your wife didn't seem to know you were a detective. She was so convincing, it made me think you were putting me on. Are you?"

"Putting you on, or a detective?"

"Either one."

"Yes," I said with a self-satisfied smile. I turned and got out of there as fast as I could.

SEVENTEEN

MY ESCAPE FROM Vivian Moloski, *La bossa*, was clean—I didn't see anyone eavesdropping.

I didn't want to answer her question—I was running a bona fide risk of having Tyranny discover my secret vocation and ruining everything. She'd blab to Daddybucks Wemple, my gassy father-in-law, and there would go my real vocation, down the test tubes, and my dependable, secure livelihood with it.

Not that that wouldn't be a blessing. But that was Gil Yates talking. Malvin Stark needed his security blanket. It was his nature to be cautious. But now the ambivalence was killing me—not to mention the jackhammer pain at the base of my skull.

Never before had I had to be both Malvin Stark and Gil Yates simultaneously. It gave me increased empathy for schizophrenics.

I was two days late for my appointment with aerobics instructor Lucy. There was no thought of attending her class, since my head and legs still ached, and I couldn't see bouncing them all over the place, as was Lucy's wont. I did sit in on the last ten minutes of class as insurance against missing her. It also gave me an opportunity to rest my bleary eyes on some healthy female bodies and ruminate on how Tyranny Rex was the largest dinosaur in the place.

"There's my aerobic animal," Lucy said in front of the whole class, just as they were disbanding. "Why didn't you join in?"

That astonished me. Certainly, in this close-knit milieu, word traveled like O.J. Simpson, and then I saw the "whoops" look on her face.

"Oh," she said, "sorry. I guess you don't feel much like jumping around."

After the place cleared out, we sat on a couple of folding chairs in the exercise room—a pleasant wooden out-building, isolated in the trees, away from the other exercise areas, which were spread all over the place. It was as though the grunting of one group might bug another group of penitents.

"Did you ever hear anything about a romance Orville Sampson had here with the boss?"

"No. When was that?"

"Fifteen or twenty years ago."

"Jeez, I was still in diapers," she exaggerated.

"Anything with a maid?"

"Orville Sampson was here for a week while I was," she said. "There was no mention of any of that stuff."

"But was there any gossip here?"

Lucy frowned. "Not with me."

"Know anyone to ask about it?"

"Jeez, Vivian, maybe—"

"I have her version already." There were a couple of birds jackassing around the trees outside. She was watching them.

"So, tell me about this shooting—" I waved at her withered arm.

"I told you—my husband was an angry man."

"What was he angry about?"

"Everything." She let go of a small, involuntary laugh.

"Specifically—when he shot you—"

"Oh, I was in his way. He'd found this rich girl he wanted to marry."

"So he tried to kill you."

"He says not. It was just a temper thing. He could have just as easily missed me. He wasn't aiming, or anything."

"Or just as easily hit you in the heart?"

She shrugged and looked back at the birds, which seemed to be engaged in a mating ritual—the male in hot pursuit of the reluctant female—who only expressed interest when the male seemed to lose it. Just like people.

"He said I got in the way of the bullet—he was just trying to scare me into backing off—"

"True?"

"He says so."

"What do you think?"

"Who knows? Jason was such a hothead. He'd do these violent, irrational things, then try to make them rational with an explanation. Blame it on someone else kind of thing."

"Jason?" I said. "His name was Jason?"

"Yeah," she said. "Popular name these days."

"Did he—did he, uh, *marry* the rich girl?"

"I wouldn't know," she said. "I put him out of my life. Oh, I tried to have him arrested—to take his guns from him—but it didn't fly."

"His last name," I said tentatively, "wasn't, by any chance, Jackson, was it?"

She looked at me as though the top of my head had been blown off. "You *know* him?"

"I know a Jason Jackson with a gun collection, middle initial is Q."

Her jaw dropped. "That's my boy. If you know his new wife, do her a favor, tell her about this—" and she waved the stunted arm at me.

"You think he could have killed Orville Sampson?"

"Why would he do that?"

"He's his father-in-law."

"No!" She swung her good hand down to slap her thigh. "I should have known. Jason could *smell* money a mile away." She shook her head. "Small world."

Yeah—and one person smaller since Orville Sampson was shot. "You think Jason's wife is in danger— for her life?"

"Yeah, well, I'd tell her not to smartmouth him, if she knows what's good for her. That boy does have a temper underneath all that phony smiling."

I thanked her for her time.

"Anytime," she said. "Now you hurry up and get well so you can come back and inspire all the girls in class."

I said I would.

On my way back to the cottage to rest before lunch, I pondered Lucy's news. Was it even possible she didn't know of the connection between Orville Sampson and her ex? I didn't figure Lucy for having a deceptive bone in her physique, but how easy is it to be wrong about people?

There was a new guard at my door—a handsome young buck who looked like he could have been a movie star. A nice contrast from all the other Pancho Villa wannabes.

"*Buenos días, señor,*" he said with a world-class smile.

And then I saw the gun.

EIGHTEEN

WAS EVERYONE IN THIS PLACE in on it? A vast conspiracy to remove Orville Sampson from this world? Why else should they be so uptight about my investigation?

The funny thing was, when I saw the gun, my first thought was not fear, but how much more difficult it would be with this newest threat to keep my secret identity from Tyranny Rex.

When the young chap waved it at me, smileless, and said, "Move," more or less, I reflected ever so briefly on the impetuosity of youth and quickly decided I would not provide an argument.

My fear shifted: did this whippersnapper know anything about firearms, or was he liable to discharge the doggie in my direction by accident? Or on purpose, actually, the result would be the same.

Since *move* was close to the Spanish word for the same thing: *mover,* I—based on the above reasoning—decided to *mover,* or move, as the case may be. In the direction he was pointing the opening at the end of the barrel of the outsized pistol he was wielding without demonstrating any aptitude for the task.

Pretty Boy took me off the property a charming back way through some pesky chaparral until we were out of sight of any fat farm-related structures. We went down a dirt road that was lined with houses a cut above hovels, but mansions they were not.

There was nothing like trudging in front of a lad with a gun at my back to heighten the pain of the last altercation I'd had with these antisocials.

After we had slogged a couple of blocks, and the jackhammer in my head was on automatic pilot, I turned and asked *"¿No carro? ¿No coche?"* meaning, more or less, "You don't have a car, Handsome?"

His stern visage led me to believe he wasn't in the mood for chitchat. But then, neither was I.

With another prod from the *pistola,* we resumed our hike. The sun was beginning to broil the sap and vinegar out of me, but I still considered it politic to play along with the charade.

Where he leads me, I will follow.

Nevertheless, I was beginning to perspire profusely and my face was beginning to feel the stingrays of the sun.

"Cerca?" I croaked. "Close?"

He didn't even grunt, causing me to wonder if he wasn't as scared as I was, and maybe I could take him—if only he hadn't had the gun. Why, I wondered, would they send a greenhorn like this out on an errand like this with a gun in his hand? Then I realized maybe my conspiracy ideas were overblown and this was a mom and pop operation. But this kid was nobody's mom or pop. I wondered if he had either. I could easily have pictured him crawling out from under one of those hot Mexican rocks with a gun already in his hand. For verily, it is said, God moves in mysterious ways.

As I felt the firecrackers exploding in my head, I wondered if this was the guy who installed the fireworks in my person. That theory would lend itself to the mom and pop hypothesis.

Just as I was wondering why someone on this street didn't see the gun and call the *policia,* I heard a male child call out, *"¿Qué pasa, José?"* and the lug behind me grunted, *"Nada."*

Nothing was happening? Moving an *hombre* down the street at gunpoint was *nothing?* I had half a mind to call out, *"Policia!"* but I pictured them halfheartedly investigating my murder if I did.

The houses abruptly stopped as we got to an area of open fields. We turned into a field and went what seemed like miles to me, but was probably more like a block or so. The field was planted in garbanzo beans, which tasted like charmless cornmeal with the high fructose taken out. Those little marble-sized balls of reconstituted sawdust, which they delighted in serving at the fat farm.

A dilapidated, windowless shed appeared and with the way the pain had increased with every step, I would have been grateful if this "José" had taken me inside and shot me.

Alas, it was not to be. He took me inside, all right, and I was instantly blinded by the darkness. I felt the presence of other people, and heard their voices distressingly close.

The shed was not large. The first thing I saw was a bunch of machetes hanging on the wall, about ten inches from my face. The barrel of the gun reposed against my ribs and the others seemed to be arguing.

A young female voice gave an excited, then muffled laugh, then spoke argumentatively.

At which my kidnapper answered back harshly. The Spanish was too fast for my blood, which seemed to have congealed to Jell-O. Looking at the machetes, I wondered if this were some kind of house of execution, and how it would feel to have my head sliced off—and how long I would feel it.

Another voice was added to the soup. This an older woman, by my reckoning, then a husky sounding man. From the size of the shed, and the cast of characters I heard, I realized they were probably all close enough to touch me—and I hoped they wouldn't.

The husky voice spoke some English—not enough, I thought, to con his way across the border—but enough for me to grasp the gist.

"Why are you here, *Señor?*"

I don't know why that struck me as funny. They

knew the answer to that better than I. "Because your *amigo* has a *pistola*—"

I could feel the tension on that metal poking me in the back, and thought perhaps humor would, under the circumstances, not be in the best of taste.

"Why do you come to Mexico?" he snapped.

"For La Puerta del Sol," I said meekly. When humble pie was called for, I sank to the occasion.

I felt the gun shoved deeper in my back, indicative, I suppose, of their lack of esteem for my answer.

"You are doing more than exercise," Grumpy grumbled.

"Well," I said, masked in my finest naïveté, "I am investigating a murder, but how could that have anything to do with you?"

The gun tightened in my ribs.

"Why are you asking about a murder in El Norte down here?"

It took me a moment to put those words in their proper order.

"Oh, well—there were telephone calls to La Puerta del Sol in the last months of his life—did he call you?" I said with a burst of *chutzpah*.

"I will ask the questions," he said to my back.

"Okay, but I can't see how any of you could have killed him, so why all this drama?"

"You are not the boss here, Americano. I will talk, you will answer. What did you come here to find out?"

"Who Orville Sampson called before he died. What he called about. To solve a mysterious murder like this, one has to find out as much as possible. Like a puzzle with many pieces."

"What do you think this pieces is?"

"I don't know," I said. "Can you help me?"

"I can help you to an early grave if you do not give me answers. What are you doing here?"

"I *told* you," I said.

"Truth! I want truth."

"Well, why don't *you* tell *me* what you think I am doing here? I really have no idea what you are afraid of."

"We are not *afraid*," he said, and I was given another disciplinary poke with the gun.

"All right," I said. "I don't know who you are, or what your connection to Orville Sampson is, but you have to admit this action is suspicious. Did one of you kill Orville Sampson?"

"No!" he almost shouted in my ear.

"Then why all this macho stuff?"

"It is not for your business."

"If you say so," I said. "All I can tell you is I had no suspicion anyone from here killed Orville Sampson. He died in Los Angeles, after all, not in Mexico—so unless one of you snuck across the border, I don't see it in the cards."

"Snuck? What is 'snuck'?"

"Crossed the border." Even as I was saying it was remote, I realized it was possible.

"What did you expect to find?"

"I don't know," I said truthfully. "A lead, a clue. I found Orville Sampson had a thing with Vivian Moloski—but that was almost twenty years ago. But he did come back before he died. But I suppose if one of you wanted to kill him, it would have been a lot easier done here."

They were silent. I broke it.

"Did one of you *want* to kill him?"

"No! He was our friend—"

Oh, I thought, now we are getting someplace. "How so?"

"That is not for your business," he said.

There was muffled talk behind my back. They began arguing. It seemed to be the young woman against the bunch. I picked up a few words, but the rush of words was beyond my understanding. *"Estupido,"* she said. She was calling them or their ideas (fears) stupid. *"No possible—"* something wasn't possible. And my favorite, *"No es fuerte el hombre,"* no strong man—I'm afraid she was referring to me.

I don't know how long they argued before I was completely exasperated.

"Look," I broke in, "why don't you just tell me what

you're worried about, and I'll tell you if you have any reason to worry—"

Thwack! That time, I heard it, followed by a female gasp, before I crumpled to the floor.

NINETEEN

WHEN MY BLEARY EYES drifted open, there was nothing in the shed but the machetes and me. For some elusive reason, I began singing, "Me and my machete," to the tune of "Me and My Shadow".

My little band of pals had dispersed to God knows where. But it couldn't have been too far—this was a small, provincial town where everybody knew everything. Which, coming to think about it, would mean even my so-called guards were in on the ruse—and if my guards were, what about the rest of the place? Vivian, and even Lucy? Both of them had connections to Orville Sampson. I was, probably, at this moment, the most *dis*connected person in town.

My trust was vaporizing, but my head was clearing. It was almost as though the second blow had nullified the first; had knocked the jackhammer out of commission. I was able to make my way back to the fat farm without that incessant pounding with every step. I don't mean I was up for Olympic competition of any sort, but the discomfort had become almost bearable.

I went right to Vivian's office, but it was locked.

People were going into the dining room, so I went looking there for Vivian. I found her at a table in the back, eating with, of all people, Lucy.

I went over to the table and fixed them with a withering glare. They didn't wither.

I unloaded my story of the afternoon. Lucy showed a touch of sympathy, but after you've been shot by your husband, how much sympathy can you be expected to work up for a bloke who's been hit on the noggin?

Vivian's reaction was more surprising. She seemed put out—like I was a nuisance. "Maybe," she said, "you'd be better off going back home. I'll refund the whole visit if you go back tomorrow."

"That's it?" I said, broadcasting my astonishment. "That's your solution? I'm knocked on the head twice, led to some shack in a bean field, at gunpoint, by someone you assigned to guard me, and your solution is for me to go home? Are you fresh out of conscience?"

"It's not that, Malvin," Lucy said, trying, I suppose, to be helpful. "There's a difficult balance here. It's no piece of cake for Vivian. The locals are glad to have the work, but after awhile, they realize they are indispensable to the operation, and we are at their mercy."

I nodded. "Nice. So they want to rough up a guest, your hands are tied?"

"It's not like that." Lucy was trying to explain without really explaining.

"Then tell me this—why is everyone so weird because I'm investigating Orville Sampson's murder? I certainly had no thought that this place was involved—" I looked at Vivian with what I thought was a devastating stare. "Now I know better."

"That's ridiculous," she said with quite a bit of conviction. "Nobody here would kill Orville Sampson. Nobody had any reason to. Oh, if you stretched it, you might say I had some motive, but that was almost twenty years ago. Now, calm down—have some dinner. Here—" she waved at an empty chair. "Join us."

Dumbfounded, I sat down. If they were hiding something, would they invite me to their table? Maybe—

"Look," I said, "I'm only going to be here for a few more days—unless I'm stuck in intensive care somewhere. I have a feeling I don't know the whole story. How about you tell me?"

"I don't know more than I've told you," Vivian said.

I searched her face for a crack. None.

"Vivian's a very honest person," Lucy said.

"And I'm hit over the head on your premises—twice—and the boss of this establishment—the mainstay of the area economy—has no idea why?" I shook my battered head. "Hard to believe."

Vivian shrugged. The waitress brought me my salad: lettuce with a nice water dressing. "Okay, if you have nothing to hide, how about letting me see your phone records—outgoing calls?"

"Fine with me," Vivian said. "I'm not sure you'll find what you're looking for. This area of the world is not noted for it's efficient recordkeeping. They send us a bill—we think it's reasonable—we pay it."

I nodded like you do when you think someone is trying to snow you. "So, let me get this straight," I said, wincing at a bite of bare lettuce. "Orville Sampson was here eighteen or nineteen years ago, trying to buy the place. You decided against selling to him. Nobody hears from him until six months before he dies. He comes back to L.A. for a couple of days and makes some calls, but no one knows to whom. Then he's shot in his bed, and you all want me to think there's nothing unusual there? Oh, and, yeah," I said, looking at Lucy, "Lucy here is shot up by her ex— who just happens to wind up married to Orville Sampson's oldest daughter. Lots of coincidences, wouldn't you say?"

"Pretty much," Lucy said with that world-class happy smile of hers. It drove me nuts.

"And *you* in this small, provincial, probably inbred community, know nothing about it?"

"Nothing," she confirmed, with a tidy shake of her head.

"Oh, *there* you are," came the inimitable voice of Tyranny Rex booming over the dining hall as she made her way like Sherman's army toward the table. "Where have you been?" she demanded on arrival, sitting herself down in the last available chair without fanfare, without being asked. It was a real conversation stopper.

"Oh, it's *you*," she said, as though noticing Vivian for the first time. "Alice in Wonderland."

Vivian looked confused, but didn't say anything. She looked as though nothing was more important to her than to be rid of us as soon as possible.

"The very idea that my husband, Malvin, was some kind of undercover private eye—why, it just boggles my mind."

I froze inside. My terror-produced stare must have tipped the girls off, for neither said anything.

"Well," Tyranny shifted gears, "I'm just having the best time at your place," she said to Vivian. "I just love it here—but don't you get island fever after a while—down here with all these Mexicans?"

"Oh, I go back to the States often," Vivian said and glanced at me with a sheepish look. "Oh, don't worry, Detective," she said, with a crooked smile, "I don't own any guns."

Lucy caressed her arm unconsciously.

"What *is* this talk?" Tyranny asked with that charmless aggressiveness she does so well.

"Dorcas is a glass blower," I blurted out. "Makes these adorable figurines: farm boys, ballerinas, cows."

Vivian looked startled; Lucy let out, then stifled, a little laugh.

Well, I thought, there goes the ball contest. I wanted

to leave, but I didn't dare leave Tyranny alone with the two of them—or it would have been goodbye cover.

So I sat through the next course: garbanzo beans on brown rice, with the husks still intact, for that bonus jolt of fiber.

Vivian and Lucy were a course ahead of me—and Tyranny a course behind—which I looked on as fortuitous, and, I could tell, so did Vivian and Lucy, for Tyranny began her glass blowing spiel, wherein she blew a lot of gas about glass.

From the look on Vivian and Lucy's faces, I knew they were wracking their brains to think of a topic they were more interested in than glass blowing. They didn't seem to be succeeding.

Both Vivian and Lucy passed on dessert and, with perfunctory pleasantries, flew out of there like birds with the same kind of feathers.

I took one bite of my garbanzo bean and brown rice entrée and decided I'd not only pass on the dessert, but on the entrée as well.

Tyranny was still going on about the vicissitudes of glass blowing when I excused myself.

I don't think she realized I was gone.

TWENTY

OUTSIDE THE DINING HALL, I had some trouble catching up with Vivian. I must have been out of breath when I wheezed, "The phone bills—where can I find them?"

"Oh, tomorrow," she said. "The accountant's gone home."

"Tonight," I said with a dose of imperialism. "I'm not going to be here that long."

She glared at me. "You're beginning to be more trouble than you're worth. My offer still goes—leave now for a full refund."

"But that wouldn't be fair to you," I said. "I must have already eaten two dollars worth of food."

"Aha! See what I mean? You aren't a good fit here."

"Thank you. Now, why don't you just show me the phone bills? You certainly know where the records are kept—"

"Because I've no idea how she files those things."

"Fine. I'll find them myself. Where are the files?"

"Oh, no," she said wearily. "I don't think so."

"Look at it this way," I said. "I get what I came for and I'll be out of your hairpiece. We drag our tootsies, no telling how much aggravation I'll be. I don't think you'd fancy me murdered on your premises. Would spread a lot of doubt about the meal fare. Headlines: 'Death by Starvation at a Fat Farm', Flash: 'Man cannot live on two calories alone'."

"If you weren't such a pain in the rear," she said, "you'd be mildly amusing. But you know, you've just made me an offer I can't refuse. In the interest of getting you and your loquacious, not to say, logorrheic wife out of my—what did you say?—hairpiece? Charming! I'm going to take you to the files. We have nothing to hide. Look at anything you want. Just try to put it all back where it came from."

She marched to the reception building, I in step right behind her.

She opened the door with a key. There was no one inside. She then led me to a closet behind the reception area. She opened the door on a bank of filing cabinets, turned on a light and peered at the square, white labels on the face of the drawers.

"Here," she said, pulling a drawer out and withdrawing a letter-sized manila folder. "Phone bills—" and she thrust the folder at me. "Have a good time. These go back almost a year."

I took the folder, and before I could express my deep gratitude, Vivian was out the door, saying, "Pull the door closed when you leave—it locks automatically." The last words were muffled in her wake.

I sat down at the receptionist's desk behind a short counter, installed, I suppose, to keep intruders at bay. I wrote down every phone call to Orville Sampson's area codes, but nothing was familiar. From the look of these bills, Orville Sampson may have called here, but no one here called him.

I replaced the folder in the drawer and perused the contents of the other drawers, my interest being piqued by the drawer that read, "Employees." I opened it to find it full of folders with names and jobs sticking up where I could see them.

My first thought, rifling through the files, was, "My, there are a lot of them." Since I didn't know what I was looking for, I decided to concentrate on employee folders marked "Housekeeping" or "Grounds-keeping" or "Kitchen."

One by one, I pulled them out of the drawer and lugged them to the desk. At first blush, it was just a bunch of names. But there were a bunch of similar ones: Gonzales, Rodriguez, Juarez. All had multiples.

On opening the folders and checking the addresses, I could separate the coincidences from the relatives.

The information was concise:

Name
Birthdate
Address

Hourly rate
Start Date

I made a list of names, addresses and birthdates, matching those with the same last names.

There were three Gonzales who lived at the same address—from the ages, it looked like a father and two sons. There was an Enrique Gonzales, forty-two, at the same address as Rosa Gonzales, thirty-seven, and an Arvilla Gonzales, eighteen, but their addresses were different. Then I found a Guadalupe Rodriguez, twenty, who lived at the same address as Arvilla. These last who worked at La Puerta del Sol for six months and two years, respectively. Rosa Gonzales had twenty years longevity, while Enrique had only fifteen years on the job. Ideas were popping in my head.

There were others with the same surnames, but their ages and addresses didn't ring any bells.

My first thought was to ask Vivian Moloski to call the three Gonzaleses and Guadalupe Rodriguez in for a confrontation. Then I thought I might be sneakier about it—if that didn't work, I could fall back on an official meeting.

I found a map of the town on the counter and checked the addresses. Both a few blocks from the farm, both in the direction of the shed, both around the corner from the other.

It was getting dark. The perfect time for stealth.

Tyranny was headed for another movie of the type featured on the telly at 3 a.m., when I stole away down the road, being careful to watch my back.

I came to the address of the elder Gonzaleses. The house was adobe (in my adobe hacienda, there's a touch of Mexico) and had one of the neater front yards on the block. Next door a vintage Chevy stood sadly on blocks in the front yard as if to say, "In my adobe hacienda, there's a touch of General Motors."

I had visions of going up to the house and hiding in the bushes, but there were no bushes. I only got close enough to see they were both in the living room watching TV—a nice, new, big screen set that seemed out of proportion to everything else inside the house or out.

The view from the back put me in mind of that honey who was eavesdropping on my conversations with Vivian Moloski—but to get a better look than her back from the neck up, I'd have to maneuver to a side window and hope I wasn't seen by anyone.

I realized her hair worked, but then I thought, so would the black hair of most Mexican women. I fancied the man one of my captors, but it was impossible to tell, since I'd never seen him.

The house wasn't at a corner—that would have been too easy. On one side was a small place, dimly lit, the other was the aforementioned junkyard. That joint was jumpin'. Where was I more likely to be noticed—on the quiet side, or the jumpin' side? Then I realized I had no choice. The living room didn't go the width of the house—the only other window was on the jumpin' joint side. My decision was made.

With a great stealth that would have made my grandmother proud, I slithered up to the property line, if there was such a thing in this shoulder of the woods. I was just approaching the living room window when I heard the crack of a rifle ring out. I must have jumped three feet in the air at the sound, and, though I didn't feel anything, I searched my body for bloodletting holes, then sank unceremoniously to the ground, where I pressed my trembling body so close to the wall, I thought I'd be mistaken for a six-foot tortilla.

Then I heard it: a grinding, throaty windup, *cghagh-aghuh,* and the explosive, propelling sound of a county fair oyster flying through the air, no doubt setting a Guinness Book world distance prize.

Another crack of the rifle, which, by this time, I realized was the front screen door, and all was quiet on the western front, save for the hell raising going on inside.

In my tortilla persona, I scootched under the living room window so I could surreptitiously rise up and glance in the window to get a look at the faces.

The reflections of the color TV tube gave a ghostly blue-green cast to the room. I caught a glimpse of the faces of the audience of two. They were hypnotized by the flickering pictures dancing in their eyes.

It was she, all right—there was no mistaking that

nosy face or that thickening body that must have once held the grace of a, an...one of those tropical birds, or animals, as the case may very well be.

I thought of storming the Bastille, but then I saw the rifle on the floor between Mom and Pop's chairs.

El Norte, where I came from, was the land of the free and the brave, and I wanted to be counted among the brave, which was why I was crawling on all fours to the street behind the houses.

I got on my feet the instant I thought it was feasible, healthwise. I checked for the second address on the damp slip of paper in my pocket (those rifle shots, cum screen door slammings wreaked havoc on the old memory). I had also drawn a little map to guide me through my miserable sense of direction.

If I reckoned correctly, the young Gonzaleses lived around the corner and down the street. I say *if* I reckoned correctly because as I made my way there, I saw I was already on the outskirts of this little town. And when I came upon the address, it turned out to be a vacant lot of generous proportions. Some trenching had been done on the lot, preparatory to building, perhaps, a Hilton hotel, from the size of it.

One thing was certain: no one was living in it, yet. There was what looked like a construction trailer in the back of the lot from which a dim gray light spilled out.

"Well," I told myself, "if you are going to be an investigator, investigate." But getting hit on the head from behind, not once, but twice, does make one wary, not to say rather cautious.

Up close, the trailer had a fading bluish cast to it. There was a hum from inside—I got the feeling you get when you are close to an occupied territory. I kept glancing over my shoulder, for obvious reasons.

I looked in the small window to a similar scene as I saw at the last stop, one generation removed. Except the distaff was solo, which put me immediately on guard for another bop on the head by the man of the house.

Where was he? The pretty young woman seemed the only one inside. I thought he could be a construction foreman here by day, and working the night shift at the fat farm.

I waited awhile to make sure the bozo wasn't hiding someplace inside. Then I knocked—gently, unthreateningly.

The young woman looked up, not frightened, but as though she were expecting her mother.

When she opened the door, her face instantly registered an awareness that I wasn't her mother. She gasped and made a gesture to close the door in my face.

"Arvilla," I said, holding my hands away from my body to demonstrate I was unarmed and harmless.

"What do you want?" she asked, the fear on her face trembling in the waves of gray light.

The thing that stopped me in my tracks and rendered me temporarily speechless was her incredible beauty. Her hair was black and shining—wavy, but not kinky. Her eyes had the luminous look of dark, moist plums, her skin a flawless light olive, her nose and lips were works of art chiseled by Michelangelo and rounded by Rodin. You think I exaggerate, but I understate.

She was dressed in a simple, straight, knee-length skirt—beige—and a white blouse, open at the neck, with no apparent effort made to hide her frontal charms.

I must have stood with my mouth agape because the first thing I remember is her mellow voice saying, "Oh, it's you." She stepped back in resignation. "I was wondering when you'd show up. You might as well come in, I guess."

I don't mean to imply her English was flawless, but, for the most part, I caught her drift. Doubtless, she had the best English among her peers, but it was, perforce, accented in the most charming manner.

I followed her inside, cautiously. "Ah, the, ah, man, the one who likes to hit people on the head. Will he be here soon?"

She smiled, and I took it like a punch to the solar plexus. She was simply a knockout.

"He's working," she said. "We can have the whole night to ourselves."

TWENTY-ONE

No way was I falling for that line. I know too good to be true when I see it, and this was it.

Cautiously, I sat in the simple chair she waved to. I started right in, before she sat in her chair, which she turned from the TV to face me. "So who down here knows Orville Sampson, and why am I being continually assaulted? What are you afraid of?"

She smiled as though we were old friends and I had told her some pleasing news.

There was something about that look—a mixture of innocence and sophistication that tickled my brain.

"We're superstitious people here—and suspicious. The others were afraid you would do us harm."

"Harm? Why? Did one of you kill Orville Sampson?"

"Oh, no, no, no," she said. "Orville was our hero. He is a god around here."

"God?"

She nodded enthusiastically. "He has been so good to us."

"Oh? How good?"

She looked startled. "You don't know?"

"I don't know what you're talking about. If he was so good, why are you afraid you will be accused of murdering him?"

"They are afraid you will take away what Orville has given us."

"What has he given you, and why would I take it away?" I was getting confused by this reasoning. "And how would I know about it?"

She looked at me slyly through a tilted eyebrow. "You are an investigator." She shrugged her pretty shoulders. "Investigators investigate."

I rubbed my head at the sentiment. I looked over at Arvilla in the half light of the TV that was blabbering away, and she took the hint, and turned off the sound, but left the picture. Then she discreetly turned on a low table lamp and turned off the TV picture.

In the brighter light she looked almost americano. Her skin was lighter, her teeth brighter, her figure sublime.

"Look at me closely," she said.

I was relieved to hear she hadn't noticed my staring. "Yes?" I said.

"Do I remind you of anyone?"

Oh, a couple movie stars, perhaps, but I didn't say anything. "Someone I know?"

"I think, yes."

My investigative mechanisms were faltering. My

eyebrows were faltering, my speech was faltering. "Well," I said, "I, ah, guess you are the daughter of Rosa Gonzales who lives around the corner, ah, down the street."

She nodded expectantly.

"She was the one listening to my conversations with Vivian Moloski at La Puerta del Sol."

She nodded again. "*Very* superstitious," she said.

"And I take it that man living with her is your father?"

Now Arvilla frowned. "I do not think I would hire you to investigate for me."

And then, as she told me, as the words were starting to form on her lips we spoke simultaneously—

"Orville was my father,"

"Orville Sampson was your father—"

You could have knocked me over with something light like bubble wrap. Then it hit me like a ton of something hard, like a Greyhound bus. "Rose is your mother?"

She smiled. "Yes, she was *very* pretty twenty years ago, you can imagine."

I couldn't imagine, but I didn't say so. The gears of my damaged brain were finally grinding, albeit at escargot pace.

"That man who lives with Rosa, what's his name? Alberto—"

"Beto, yes he is her husband. But I was three years old when they were married. I always thought of him as my father. I have his last name," she smiled, "but I have someone else's first name."

"Of course, Arvilla," I said, the light dawning. "How did you find out? About Orville Sampson?"

"He came back here. He was looking for something. I don't know what. Perhaps my mother, perhaps something else. I don't know—"

"How did he find you?"

"I was his maid. For his room, I mean. I was making his bed when he came back from breakfast. I don't think he went to many exercise classes. The moment he saw me he stopped dead and stared at my face. His jaw dropped." She giggled. "So he saw himself in me even if you didn't."

"I'm sorry," I said. "I should have."

"We got to talking. He asked me a thousand questions. And, of course, he saw my mother in my face, too."

I couldn't. That puffy, dumpy woman did not put me in mind of this raving beauty in the least. Of course, that's a sentiment I wouldn't dare express to anyone, lest I be accused of being a horrible sexist.

"And who is hitting me over the head?"

She blushed. "I tried to get him not to."

"Your boyfriend? The guy who lives here with you?"

She nodded.

"What's *he* got against me?"

"It is misplaced macho—chivalry. He thinks you can take away what Orville gave us."

"What was that?"

"Money," she said sheepishly, as though she were sharing an off-color story with a stranger.

The old lights were going on in that battered noggin of mine. Here is where the money went! But, so much? "A lot of money?"

"Oh, yes," she said. "More than any of us could imagine. More than all of us could make in a lifetime—"

"Yet your mother still works? Your boyfriend, too?"

"And my father, and me."

"Why?"

"I told you. We are a superstitious people. We think such good fortune might be followed by bad fortune. We are afraid to quit our jobs, which gave us a comfortable living, in case something bad happens, and we can't get them back."

"Like what bad?"

"Oh, the bank where the money is burns down, or is robbed, or we are kidnapped, or something, and have to pay ransom."

I shook my head. "Where is the bank?"

"It is in your country. They send us money every month."

"How much money?"

She blushed again. "I am ashamed to tell."

"Why?"

"I did nothing for it."

"Your mother did."

"Yes, but the money is in my name." Tears began to frame her pretty eyes. "He said…" she halted her speech to sniffle, then blow her nose. "I was…the most wonderful…thing…he ever did, and—oh, I can't say more—"

"Why not?"

"It is too embarrassing. He didn't know me, but he said he loved me…more…than his North American daughters. I was, what did he say? Not spoiled? Is that correct?"

I nodded. "And I'm sure he meant it," I said. "Did Orville tell you why he wanted to do this when he did? Why did he come here in the first place—last year?"

"Not directly, no."

"Indirectly?"

She frowned. "My mother and I, we thought Orville thought he was…going to die soon. It was nothing he said exactly, so much as a feeling we got. We could have been wrong, but it turned out we were not."

"Yeah—"

"And we were very lucky he put the money in the bank before he died. From what he told us of his children, they certainly wouldn't have given up a million dollars, even though I hear they had many times that."

"A million?" I said, astonished, but not for the obvious reason. That accounted for two thirds of Orville's last minute cash withdrawals, but not for the other five hundred thousand dollars.

"Do you know of anyone else he might have given money to?"

"No," she said. "He did not speak to me about others."

"Do you think he might have had other unknown children?"

She shrugged. "The way he was so happy about me, I don't think so."

"Before I go," I said, "I want to assure you that your money is probably very safe in the bank it's in. We have government insured bank accounts, and I'm sure Orville Sampson was careful with how he handled yours. But if you will tell me the name of the bank, I'll check on it for you and write to you what I find out—"

Arvilla seemed to go stiff, like she'd just gotten a jolt of *rigor mortis*.

"Oh, don't worry, I'm not going to steal the money. I just want to reassure you. But, if you don't want to tell me, it's okay—"

"Are you sure you are not here for the family of daughters to get the money back?"

"Yes, I'm sure. I've met Orville Sampson's daughters and their husbands—creepy—and Orville was right. You are the only one of his daughters that's a real person—you're the best of the lot. Not spoiled, not idle. You have lots of money and you are still working. I don't work for the daughters."

"Who do you work for?"

"Orville's widow. There is a clause in his will that his money can't be distributed until his murder is solved."

She looked confused. "How can that be? How could he know he was going to be murdered?"

I shrugged. "I don't know. I think it was just a suspicion. If you met his sons-in-law, that suspicion might be justified."

"So no one is getting their money until you find the murderer?"

"That's right. Any ideas?"

"Oh, no. I don't know those people."

"Orville gave you no background on them?"

"No. Just to say they were all spoiled and took him for granted."

"Say, is there any chance your boyfriend will come back with an axe and split my head open?"

She covered her eyes with her hand. "I will tell him you are not taking our money away."

"Are you going to marry him?"

"He wants to. But now that this has happened, I wonder if he only wants to marry me because of the money."

I smiled at that, then shook my head. "No," I said, "I think you have some other things going for you."

"Going for me?"

"Yes, good qualities to attract a man other than money. Look how you charmed Orville Sampson. He was a tough business man, and you won his heart. Say, what is going on outside—the digging? It looks like someone is building."

"Yes, we are building a house."

"Wow," I said. "Big—"

"Yes, big for here, but little next to the money I have been given. It is so much money, I don't know how to spend it all. A nice car we don't need; we can walk to work. A yacht—we are too far from the ocean. An airplane? Where would we go? Besides, we do not want to make our neighbors jealous. Our house will be simple, but it will be more than the others have and it could make hard feelings."

I nodded. I loved her for her simple wisdom. I could see why Orville settled a million on her. I only wonder why he didn't give her more. But, as she explained, what would she do with more? It might have turned her into a Sampson girl.

I stood and thanked her for her honesty. "Please tell your boyfriend and mother and—father?—her husband I am your friend. No harm will come to your money because of me."

"Thank you," she said, and she seemed to have had a burden lifted from her back. She stood, too. "Do you want me to show you what our house will be?"

"I'd like that," I said, slapping on my face a smile of my own.

We went outside and she pointed out with *mucho* pride where the living room, dining room and kitchen were going to be. Then the bedrooms, three to start. "We can build on later, if we need to." She was blushing again.

I expressed my gratitude for her showing me the house layout, and my awe at her good nature and beauty.

"So, I guess the telephone calls were to you—"

"My mother, mostly," she said. "She helped with setting up the money, I guess."

Ah, there it was again—the money. I sure would love to have the name of the bank. It could offer a clue to what happened to the other five hundred grand, but I'd decided I wasn't going to push her for it.

I took her hand in mine and said goodbye—and wished her all kinds of good fortune for the future.

"I appreciate that," she said.

As I turned to go, she spoke to my back— "It's Bank of America in San Diego. The downtown branch."

The warmth started in my ears, bounced around there for a bit, then swam through my body like a shot of Tequila.

I turned to look at her. I nodded my thanks. We were both smiling.

TWENTY-TWO

TYRANNY REX was reading in bed when I got back. She looked my way when she heard the door open.

"Where in the world were you?" she asked.

"Oh," I said impulsively, "out doing my usual detective work," and we both had a good laugh, though I would characterize her laugh more as a guffaw.

She went back to her book. My answer, if it had registered, seemed to satisfy. That was Tyranny. She'd ask a small talk question and any collection of sounds would satisfy for the answer, as though she tuned out as soon as the question was asked.

Meanwhile, things were heating up in *El Norte*. Next morning, I called my message service to hear the groggy voice of Pamela Sampson with the news: "Gil? I just got out of intensive care. Kurt sicked his dogs on me and they almost tore me apart. I'm lucky to be alive—I think. The way I feel, I'm not so sure living is that appealing." She clicked off without giving me the details. Not even the hospital.

Later that morning, I hung around outside Vivian Moloski's office, and it was only a matter of minutes before Arvilla's mother appeared. She had a new smile on her face. Her English was almost nonexistent, but between my gardener's Spanish and her hotel English, we managed.

She told me Orville Sampson, in those brief moments, was the love of her life, a fact she shared with her daughter, but not with her husband. They were deathly, if not irrationally, afraid that I would spoil it all. They didn't mean to hurt me, just to keep me off balance. Scare me, so if I had any notions of taking the money from them, they had the ability to remove me.

"How did you get together again after twenty years?"

"He came back," she said, "to help his body get well."

"What was wrong with his body?"

"He had cancer, he told me. He did not come to see me—I was just still here. He said he didn't expect I would be. He had no idea I had his child. He wanted to meet her. He was excited. When he met her, he fell in love all over." She blushed. "I used to look like her."

I'm afraid she caught me staring. I could see some lines of resemblance, but the Mexican country life had sapped the beauty out of her.

"He thought she was so nice. So different from his other daughters, he was just enchanted. He said he was going to send money—we never asked for a peso."

"How old were you?"

"I was only sixteen. I looked older. I told him I was,

but, the way he looked at me, it wouldn't have mattered him *how* old I was. I could have been fourteen.

"He asked me if I had birth control. I told him *sí,* but it was not the truth. I was a good Catholic girl, and I wouldn't use birth control if my church didn't want me to. I guess to my confused young mind, lying was not as big a sin."

"So he came back here in the hopes a fat-free diet and exercise would help him?"

"Yes, and that is part of it. The other part is a doctor in town who does things doctors in the states can't."

"Oh? Where can I find him?"

"Dr. Sanchez, Alberto Sanchez. I will tell you how to get there..."

Tyranny was, fortunately, taking to the exercise regimen at La Puerta del Sol like a duck to champagne. After lunch—fresh fruit, bare baked potatoes, tofu sandwiches garnished with bean sprouts—take your pick. If you ever had a baked potato with nothing on it, or a tofu sandwich on seven grain bread, you'd do what I did—the fresh fruit. Tyranny headed for another session of lifting her gams in the swimming pool. I headed in the direction of Dr. Sanchez.

His building was just around the corner from the truncated main drag. It was an unpainted wooden book that looked not unlike one of those saloons in a horse opera.

The waiting room looked much like the unpainted boards of the outside. Tough times for interior decorators. But the room was swimming in gringoes, with just a smattering of Mexicans.

The receptionist sat behind a chin-high counter. She was young and perky—just having graduated from San Diego State and returned home to do good.

I'm speculating, of course, but her faculty for English could not have been picked up south of the border.

"Do you have an appointment?" She smiled at me with a set of choppers that bespoke a salubrious bean diet.

"No…I'm…"

"That's all right," she said easily. "We'll fit you in, if you don't mind waiting."

"I don't mind—"

"Good. Have a seat—if you can find one."

"How long do you figure?"

"You never know. Doctor cares very much for his patients. He can take a long time." She looked around the waiting room and shrugged.

I thanked her, sat in the last available chair and waited.

And waited.

I was about to wilt from the heat in the densely populated, unairconditioned waiting room. I passed time trying to scope out my fellow waiters.

Every now and then, someone came out and another was called in. The turnover rate was not what you'd call *rapido*.

On my left was a hefty gringo woman. On my right,

a grumpy looking man who looked so old, I wondered why he wanted to hang on any longer. May have been Mexican in origin—gringo in dress. I decided to take my chances with the female.

"Where you from?"

"Texas," she said. "El Paso."

"Been here before?"

"Lord, yes," she said. "Every chance I got. I've got cancer in my boobs," she said, looking down at the Himalayas.

"Is Dr. Sanchez doing you any good?"

"Well, Lord, yes, I should say so, or I wouldn't be coming back."

"May I ask why you come all this way?"

She looked at me askance. Were my screws unhinged? "Same reason's you, I expect. We can't get this stuff in the U.S.; Food and Drug people draggin' their feet. What can you expect from the folks who blew up that cult down home to hell and gone?"

"Wasn't that the department of alcohol, tobacco and firearms?"

"All the same, you ask me."

Perhaps it was a mistake to take her word—

"Lot cheaper, too," she said.

I nodded. She opened her yap for another salvo, but, luckily, her number was up and she jumped, as best she could, and wiggled into the inner sanctum. The waiting room was thinning out somewhat.

I wasn't sanguine about getting in to see the witch doctor before dinnertime.

But I made it. Dr. Sanchez was an older guy—not the look of one you'd think was up to date on all the latest. He was bent over his desk furiously writing notes.

"Yes, sir?" he said in English—not as good as the receptionist, but easily understandable.

I introduced myself. "I'm not sick," I said up front. "I wonder if you remember Orville Sampson from the U.S.? Very rich."

He frowned. "A lot of people come and go here everyday." He seemed to be thinking, searching for a memory jog.

"He was murdered," I said. "I'm trying to find out who—and why."

The doc frowned again. "Don't know I can help you. I didn't do it."

"I'm sure. I just wondered what he was doing here."

He looked at me through his eyelashes, without lifting his head. "People come here sick," he said.

"You cure them?"

"Some. Even *Dios* doesn't hit one hundred percent."

"Your number's high?"

Now the head tilted up. "You think I'm a fake? A witch doctor?"

"Doesn't matter what I think. From the look of your waiting room, you don't seem to be hurting for believers."

"Faith? You think I'm a faith healer?"

"What do you think you are?"

"My dream is to be a healer. Heal the sick. I don't much care how I do it."

"Whatever works?"

He nodded, suspiciously.

"What did you do for Orville Sampson? Faith or medicine?"

"Probably both. That's my goal. Let me look him up. See if I have anything on him—spell the last name, please."

I did so as he pawed through a filing cabinet behind his desk. He pulled out a battered manila envelope, opened it, and spread it on his rough hewn desk and peered at it.

"Oh, yes, now I remember him. Prostate cancer."

"Terminal?"

"The diagnosis from his personal doctor in Los Angeles was wavering. Near as I can tell, it was fifty-fifty. I gave him Benefin."

"What's that?"

"It's a powder made out of shark cartilage."

"That works?"

He nodded with an engaging gravity. "Sharks don't get cancer," he said, "isn't that something?"

"I don't know, is it?"

"The results have been encouraging."

"You know how Orville Sampson responded to it?"

The doctor looked back in the file. "He was only here twice—five days apart."

"Is that normal?"

"Normal? I'm here to serve. If someone wants to come once, it's okay. Everyday—okay, too. I deal in hope."

"Hope?" I asked skeptically. "Not very scientific."

He shrugged. "Best science in the world in the United States."

I must have looked alarmed.

"You ever been diagnosed with cancer?"

"No—"

He nodded as though he expected the answer. "So, I don't imagine you can relate to someone whose doctor told him he was going to die. You try everything. Good as your science is, doctors are often wrong. They're just people. I have medicine they can't have. I believe with medicine your mind has to work *for* you, too. One without the other—" He threw up his hands.

"You're talking voodoo—" I said.

"Some people believe in voodoo. What do you believe in, Mr. Yates?"

"I…"

"When you see your life slipping away, not everyone turns their backs on the unknown. Would you?"

Would I? I wondered. "How did you leave it with Orville Sampson?" I asked. "After his second visit?"

"Leave it? I listen, I look, I prescribe. If I don't see

someone again, I assume one of two things—either I cured them, or…" He stopped. I didn't need to ask the other, but I did.

"Or?"

"Or they died."

One thing I could bank on. The shark fin powder wasn't what killed Orville Sampson.

TWENTY-THREE

THE ASSAULTS STOPPED COLD after my chat with Arvilla; so I devoted the rest of the week to healing and thinking. The former came easier. I had learned a lot about the character of Orville Sampson, but nothing about why anyone would murder him. Certainly, none of these people to whom he had been so generous. I had accounted for a million of the 1.5 million in cash Orville Sampson went through in his last days. Could this million or that half have caused his death? Did one of his kids get wind of it and panic—afraid Orville would blow it all? It seemed so hard to believe that anyone who could count wouldn't have realized what a drop in the spittoon a million and a half was. By my reckoning, it was one one-thousandth of his net worth. Like spending a hundred bucks if you happened to be worth one hundred thousand. Nothing to make a fuss about. Could someone have feared this was only the beginning of a huge hemorrhage of money that had to be nipped at the early flowering stage? Sometimes, fear knows no logic—perhaps all the time.

But there was no evidence anybody knew anything about these late gifts.

Would another phone number lead me to the remaining half mil? And would it be significant? Or was that stipend perhaps frittered away a nickel at a time?

When I said goodbye to Vivian Moloski at the end of the week, I'd never seen anyone so glad to see me leave.

It was a long shot to visit the San Diego bank where Orville Sampson had stashed the cash for his daughter—but there was the matter of the missing five hundred grand to contend with and I'd love to have a fix on that, no matter how remote my chances were of getting that from a bank.

I told Tyranny I wanted to stop off and see one of my favorite palm and cycad dealers in San Diego— "You want to go along, or shall I drop you at a shopping center?"

She made what I have come to recognize as the palm and cycad face—prickly as the spines on an *Encephalartos horridus*.

It was a good thing she chose the shopping center, or else I'd have had to go to the palm guy instead of the bank. I gave her ninety minutes when I dumped her, then headed for the bank downtown.

I'd hoped the big cheese would be a woman. One who just couldn't resist my pretty blue eyes.

I got half my wish. The Big Cheese was a bratwurst. My first thought was if she stood up, the chair would stand with her.

I smiled a smile I didn't even know I had in me, and

sank into the chair facing the sign, "Cindy Manoff, Manager". One of those chocolate and beige plastic wonders that lends so much credibility to the job without costing an arm and an eyeball.

"My, you have gorgeous…eyes," I said, not having sufficient confidence to say, "Blue". They might have been green, in which case, I might have been in the gazpacho.

She tried to compete with my fulsome smile, but didn't come close.

"Gil Yates," I said, not taking my eyes off her eyes. She shifted them somewhat.

"Who is that?" she said.

"Me," I said.

"Do you have an account here, Mr. Yates?"

There it was, on the table, up front. You have any dough? Do we get to use it?

We sparred a while. I told her I was investigating the murder of one of their depositors and all the family would appreciate any information she could share. I told her I knew of the million dollar account and how there was a missing half million—and was that, by any chance, parked in her bank?

"Mr. Gates, is it?"

"Yates."

"Oh, Yates—yes—the cowboy on *Rawhide*—" (you get recognition from the strangest people.) "The

Clint Eastwood part. How charming. But our bank records are confidential."

"I suppose we could go through the mess of a subpoena."

"Then that's what you'll have to do."

Cat and catnip. "Okay, Cindy," I said. "But to save us all the fuss and bother, couldn't you just flash up on that screen of yours the name Orville Sampson and see if anything comes up. You don't have to tell me what it is. Just tell me if there is another account worth subpoenaing."

The bratwurst stared at me for a moment. I'm sure the old gears were turning over what the chances were. I'm also sure that the guy who set up the million dollar account for a pretty, young Mexican girl would not be soon forgotten, and if he'd dumped another five hundred thousand on them, it would be stuck in the old memory bank, and searching the computer screen would be superfluous.

But search she did. She pursed her lips, furrowed her brow and frowned. "Nothing," she pronounced.

"Under Orville Sampson?" I asked.

"Correct."

"If he had given the money to someone else to put in here, would there be a record?"

"Not under his name—unless it was vested 'In trust for…'"

"Did you handle the million dollar transaction for Orville Sampson and Arvilla Gonzales?"

"I did—"

"Do you remember any other transactions around that time—involving Orville Sampson?"

"Not that I recall," she evaded.

"Recall. Do you do a lot of transactions of that magnitude?"

"Not a lot, but there are others."

"Do you remember Orville Sampson mentioning any other deposits?"

"As I told you, the bank records are confidential. But perhaps I can save you some trouble. That million dollar deposit was the only one he made, to my knowledge. My screen shows no other."

"Thanks, Cindy," I said, though I didn't feel so grateful.

I had time to stop by the Palm and Cycad King of San Diego and picked up an *Encephalartos macrostrobilis* seedling for a hundred bucks. It would lend credence to my cover.

At a gas station phone booth, I checked my messages again, in the hope my client would tell me what hospital she was in—or at least that she was alive.

Hard for her to pay a fee if she wasn't.

There was only one message. It was from Kurt Roberts.

"Gil, Kurt Roberts here. I suppose you've heard the news. I just want you to know it's not what it seems. Give me a call, if you want to talk about it."

Rather drop in on him. Maybe I'd get lucky and he wouldn't be home. I expect that roving wife of his would be most cooperative.

In the meantime I had to steel myself for the return voyage with the indomitable Tyranny Rex.

I only had to wait twenty-five minutes in the shopping center parking lot until she showed up, so laden with packages I could barely see her.

The sight of her staggering under her load caused ideas to sweep through my brain:

1. It is a good thing I only bought the cycad seedling. There wasn't room for anything else in that cheesy car Daddy Pimple provided me for a company car.

2. I would have saved a lot of money taking her with me to the bank and blowing my cover.

3. I *needed* the cover to pay for all the junk she bought while I was maintaining my cover.

4. My cover was secured by her purchases. She could talk about them the entire two and a half hours of the return trip.

When I helped her stash her burden in the trunk and backseat, dwarfing and shading my *Encephalartos macrostrobilis*. She said, "I've just found the most wonderful things."

"Tell me about them," I said.

TWENTY-FOUR

WHILE TYRANNY TALKED on the way home, I outlined my plan of attack in the Sampson case. Over the years, I had developed this skill of hearing without listening. While Tyranny talked, I thought. We were both happy.

Back at the feet of the omnipotent Elbert August Wemple, Realtor Ass., his first words were, "You don't look in any better shape than when you left."

"Well, I…"

"Just another goldbricking operation. 'Bout time you do an honest day's work, you ask me."

I didn't ask him. I stared at him. It was a heavy dandruff day in those quarters.

He blathered on, but I wasn't listening. We had a ball of snakes over on Park Street, he was saying, but I had my own ball of snakes. Tuning out the whole Wemple clan made excellent sense.

I nodded at a few propitious moments, then sat down at my desk and picked up the phone. The gasbag on the platform in front of me would think I was doing his bidding while I was stoking my own fires.

Fortunately, I was calling within our area code. Daddy Dandruff personally checked the phone bills for long distance calls.

First, I called Pamela Sampson at home, in the hope she had been released from the hospital. No answer.

Dilemma: which offspring to call first? The guy who put her there had left me a message already, and I didn't want to get his story on the phone, I wanted to look him in the eye—not that appealing a prospect, but it had to be done.

Gorberg was out of the question. He wouldn't tell the truth to save his soul. I'm not sure he knew how.

Jason Q. Jackson was the last resort. But now that I knew he'd shot an ex-wife (and there could have been six of them), it gave me pause.

Oh, well, I thought, maybe his wife will answer.

Wrong.

"Ho!" he said on answering. It was a macho-friendly greeting.

"Ho!" I said in return. "Gil Yates here. I understand Pamela had a little mishap."

"Phuh!" He must have sprayed the mouthpiece with a gallon of spittle. "That stupid Roberts and his dogs. *No*body is safe around 'em."

"Know what hospital she's in?"

"Hold on a minute—Francine! What hospital is Pam in?" I couldn't hear her response, but he was back on the line with it. "St. John's—Santa Monica."

"Thanks," I said and hung up—minimizing my contact with the smiler.

I pulled into the parking lot of St. John's around dinnertime.

Pamela had a nice private room. She was sitting up in bed attempting to cope with some institutional viands on a tray in front of her. She was heavily bandaged, but able to locomote the food to her mouth—not, from the look of it, a joyous task.

"Gil!" she said on looking up. "Am I glad to see you. Where have you been? He tried to *kill* me," she said as though she still found that surprising.

I sized her up quickly to ascertain if she could take the news. I decided she could. "I've been to Mexico."

"Mexico?"

"Yes. I followed the leads on the phone bill. To cut to the chaser, your husband, Orville, fathered a child there."

"No!"

"Oh, not in your time—twenty years ago. He found out quite by accident when he went south for a miracle cure."

"Cure? What *is* this?" Her eyes were narrow, but brimming with suspicion.

I shrugged as though it weren't important. "Apparently he had cancer."

"Oh, Gil," she said, as though relieved, "you know Orville was such a hypochondriac."

"Well, it's academic, anyway. It wasn't the cancer that killed him."

"No, it was Kurt Roberts—and he tried to kill me, too. Oh, why don't you sit down, Gil—there's a chair here someplace—there it is," she said, pointing to the corner next to the TV set.

For some reason, I didn't feel much like sitting. I did it in deference to Pamela's disposition. "Tell me what happened—"

"He came to the house with those wretched dogs of his." She shuddered at the memory, giving up all pretense of eating. I wanted to tell her, bad as hospital food was, she should count her blessings she wasn't at a fat farm.

"On what pretense did he bring his dogs to your house?"

She waved a hand, which I understood to mean to dismiss what she was going to say as unimportant. "Just call it a friendly visit."

"Did it turn out friendly?"

"No, it did *not!*" She winced at the pain, or the memory, or both.

"Had he ever brought the dogs to you before?"

"No. *Never!* I should have known that he was up to no good."

"Kurt had been a frequent visitor to your house, had he not?"

"Oh, he came around some, sure. We might even

have had a dalliance for a while. Okay, I'll admit it. But I always had the sense he was using me."

"For what?"

"Info about Orville. Now I think he was vicariously stalking him. Maybe he was afraid I knew too much."

"But what did you know?"

"I knew he was a sneaky little opportunist. But *this!*"

"What happened?"

"He came to see me—said he was just driving home from dog training and decided to drop by—" Her face showed her low evaluation of that statement. "So he pretends to be all excited about the new tricks his dogs have learned and he wants to show me."

She paused as though the idiocy was sinking in all over again. "Well, I hadn't the least desire to see his doggies roll over and play dead, or whatever his tricks were supposed to be, but he looked so hurt at my refusal that I felt sorry for him, and I went out there. He was parked in the driveway out front, and I could tell his dogs were sorely agitated, the way they were jumping around in the car. I even said to him, 'It looks like they're angry, or hungry, or something. I don't think you should let them out.'"

"What did he say?"

"He pooh-poohed it. Said they didn't like to be cooped up. As soon as they were out, they'd calm down.

"Well, I wanted none of it, so I turned and started back to the house, and I heard the car door open, and

Kurt gave them some command, and even without looking, I knew what was happening. He'd brought those dogs to kill me. I heard a *whoosh* as they flew through the air to get me. There were three of them and before I knew it, I was flat on the ground and those beasts were tearing at my flesh with their horrible, sharp teeth. I struggled, flailed my arms, tried to get them off me."

"What was Kurt doing?"

"Nothing! He was making believe he was shocked, but he didn't do anything to stop them till he thought I was dead. Then one sharp word from him, and they stopped dead. He thought I was unconscious. Dead! Well, I almost *was*. When he saw my eyes were half open, he apologized profusely. 'Oh, I'm so sorry—I don't know what got into them. They were so good at school.' I didn't buy it for a minute."

"Did you call the police?"

"Are you kidding? I couldn't move."

"How did you get here?"

"Kurt brought me."

"So he didn't leave you there for dead?"

"Not when he saw I was alive. Anyway, the hospital calls the police. I think they have to report dog bites."

"Some bite," I said, looking at her smothering bandages.

"Yeah, and you ain't seen nothing, yet. You don't want to see my body—what's left of it."

"So what's your theory? Why did he get inspired to do this all of a sudden?"

"There's the question, of course," she said. "Don't think I haven't had time to think that one over! He wanted to kill me, that's all I'm sure of. Why? Obviously, his share would increase, but more probably, he was afraid you'd find out he was guilty and killing me would take you out of the picture. I don't suppose you'd work without being paid?" It was a question.

"Not likely," I said.

"He's the one I'd look to. Didn't I tell you he was a weasel?"

"You did."

"To top it off, he had the nerve to come in here with his wife, Orville's daughter, and express the most bogus sympathy and contrition you ever saw in your life. Said he told the police how sorry he was, what an unfortunate accident it was—"

"And they bought it?"

"They bought it. Hook, line, and sinker. Weasel! He's your man, Gil. Sic 'em!"

TWENTY-FIVE

NEXT STOP: KURT ROBERTS.

All that grass once again put me in mind of Orville Sampson and the Forest Lawn cemeteries. May he rest in peace. And may these other bozos have no peace until I rest my case.

Lolly answered the door, God bless her. She seemed startled to see me, and not a little afraid.

"Oh, Mr. Yates," she said. "I hope you didn't get the wrong idea the other day—"

"What *is* the wrong idea?"

"Well," she said, wringing her hands and shrugging her shoulders, "you know…"

"You mean I might think you were serious about becoming a Mormon?"

She looked at me with one eye closed, as though that open eye was telescoping my soul. Could she really hope I was that stupid? She seemed to relax a mite, indicating that she thought I was that stupid. She wasn't the first…

"I'm just here to see Kurt. He called me."

"Oh, I'll get him," she said, vastly relieved.

"I understand the dogs got quite a feast on Pamela Sampson—" I stopped her.

"Yes," she said with a frown, then trotted out the party line that Kurt was so upset about it. "They just went crazy on him—"

"Yeah," I said. "Real crazy…"

"Um hum," she said, revealing the first skepticism, then looking over her shoulder to make sure she wasn't being understood.

At that moment, hubby Kurt came bounding into the room as though he were on a slightly out-of-kilter pogo stick.

"Yates, there you are," he said as though he'd been looking all over for me. If he'd seen my car out front, why would he be surprised to find me in his house? He seemed a little nervous in that overingratiating way. He was almost a midget version of his brother-in-law, Jason Q. Jackson. Both were world class smilers.

"Well," he said with disarming good nature, "I hope you didn't get the wrong idea about that little incident out at Pamela Sampson's—"

Hardly "little," I thought, but I said, "What was the right idea?" *Déjà vu* all over again.

"I was coming from the dog training program on Saturday morning. Pamela's was on the way, and I thought I'd drop in and see how she was doing. I know she's been lonely since Orville died—" I saw him steal the barest glance at his wifey to see if she was buying it the second time. Way I heard it, Kurt was keeping Pamela company even while Orville was alive.

"Where did you take the dogs for training?" I asked, so low-key, unsuspiciously, I surprised even myself.

He answered readily: "Dog's Discipline over on Sawtelle," he said. "So while I was over at the Sampson's, I thought I'd show Pamela one or two tricks they'd learned."

"What were they?"

"Oh." He blushed. "Nothing fancy. Just heeling and rolling over and stuff like that."

"Did you have to give them some command to perform?"

"Yeah, sure. But as soon as I opened the door to let them out of the car, they took off for Pamela like there was no tomorrow."

"You try to stop them?"

"Well, of course, I did. Certainly."

"How?"

He shot me a look that told me without telling me he was a bit out of joint at me questioning him. Especially since the real answers were not that convincing. The answers he gave didn't cement my belief in his veracity.

"Well, I commanded them to heel."

"How do you do that?"

"Just shout, 'Heel!'"

"Did they heel?"

"No, that was the strange thing. I couldn't stop

them. Well, it was their first class and they did just fine at the school, and I didn't have any idea those puppies would flip out like that—"

I nodded in the hope of camouflaging my skepticism. I looked out back at the "puppies." More like ponies, I thought. The three of them were scampering around, baring their teeth in the most uninviting manner. They looked famished. Was it my imagination, or were they looking my way?

I looked at Lolly and saw her sublimated terror. We were both thinking the same thing. When would Kurt turn the dogs on us?

Kurt was shaking his head. "Jeez, the cops were here and everything, like I had sicked the pups on her on purpose."

"Didn't?"

"*Heck,* no—"

"Just to scare her a little, maybe? Got out of hand?"

"No. No, *no!*"

"Cops believe you?"

"Who knows?" he said in what seemed to me a burst of disarming candor. "I haven't heard from them. My word against hers kind of thing, I guess."

"She told a different story?"

"Apparently." He shrugged so I would understand he had no *real* knowledge of what she said. "You know cops," he explained, "always trying to throw you off balance."

"What did she tell them?"

"Oh, it's too ridiculous to repeat," he said.

"I can take ridiculous," I prodded.

"Well." He shrugged and shook his head. "Told them I sicked the dogs on her and I didn't do anything to stop them until I thought she was dead." He sighed. "I called the paramedics, for crying out loud." He shook his weasel head again as though the whole thing was too crazy for words. He pulled a mile-long face. Then he sighed, "They destroyed my dogs." He looked so sad I almost felt sorry for him. I looked out back at the three dogs, then at Kurt. "Oh, I replaced them right away," he said. Kurt's eyes flinched at a sudden thought. "Say," he said, "where you been? I called you as soon as this happened. It's been almost a week."

"I was in Mexico," I said, checking his reaction. Nothing.

"Oh, have a good time?"

"Off and on," I said. "I didn't go for a good time."

"Oh? Business?"

I didn't want to make him beg. "Yes. Did you know about Orville's Mexican connection?"

From the look of him, he didn't. Would he try to bluff? "Orville had connections all over the world," Kurt said. "No one could keep up with all of them." He paused. "Anything interesting?"

"I think so," I said casually—no sense exciting the

Robertses. "Orville fathered a child in Mexico—around twenty years ago."

Lolly looked surprised. Kurt shrugged his shoulders.

"He settled a million dollars on her." I dropped it while checking their faces. Now Kurt was more surprised than Lolly.

"A million bucks! You can buy all of Mexico with that," he said. "Oh, she'll probably blow it all on jai alai, or something."

"No," I said. "It's an annuity. She gets so much a month."

"Jeez, must be about four or five grand a month on the interest alone."

"The mystery is there's another five hundred thousand in cash unaccounted for."

"Don't look at me," Kurt said. "I didn't get it."

"Any ideas?"

"Imagine that was petty cash to Orville," he said.

"Did you know he had cancer?" I asked Lolly.

"Oh, Dad always had something. He *was* a hypochondriac, after all. I remember when I was a kid, he had a mole or something cut off his face, and the doctor called it a cancer. It was a harmless thing, but dad went around like it was terminal. Then, later he got prostate cancer. Same thing—scary word, but not fatal. Couldn't tell him that."

"He went to Mexico for treatment. Did you know that?"

"No. We didn't know much after the suit was filed. He walled us off—even those who didn't sue," she said with a pointed look at her hubby.

"Hey!" Kurt shifted gears. "Come on out back, I'll show you both what the new pups can do." I loved the way he downplayed the beasts' viciousness.

Lolly and I looked at each other.

"Jeez, sorry," I said. "I've got to run. Maybe another time…"

He looked genuinely disappointed as I high-tushed it out of there.

I'd have to let Lolly look out for herself.

TWENTY-SIX

DOGGIE DISCIPLINE, over on Sawtelle, in West L.A. was staffed by those horsey looking young girls who have given their hearts and souls to the animal kingdom. I don't know what it was about them, but you saw them anywhere you saw animals. The type that kept lions or rattlesnakes in their bedrooms, curried horses or trained monkeys.

My first question was why Kurt drove so far for Doggie Discipline. There must have been closer spots. This was probably the closest to the Bel Air Manse of Pamela and the late Orville Sampson. Though it wasn't "on the way," as Kurt advertised.

"Hi, I'm Jennifer," said the earnest young damsel in jeans and a sweatshirt that must have been peach before it faded.

I saw Jennifer was the kind of woman who had more time for animals than people, so I closed in on the chase. "Guy here last weekend with three Dobermans. Short guy. Remember him?"

"Sure. Nice guy. Seemed so, anyway," she said after

looking at my reaction. I must be careful with that; I don't want to influence anyone with a look.

"So what did he want to train his dogs to do?"

"Control. He wanted control so he could have them attack at an instant, quiet command, and, by the same token, keep them from attacking."

"Hmm—make progress?"

"Yes. The dogs were very receptive."

"Teach them to roll over—anything like that?"

She laughed. "Dobermans? Not likely. You want holy rollers, you go for something like a Collie. Lassie was a good roller."

I thanked Jennifer for her help and headed back to Torrance and that Realtor, Ass., my father-in-law.

I found him out to lunch. Not that unusual when you think of it. Even when he was sitting the two steps above me, he was out to lunch.

I called my messages. I had one from Rolf Gorberg.

"Yates? Rolf Gorberg. You won't believe this—I'm in the slammer. Some stupid mistake, but the boys in blue aren't budging. Thought you might help me out— knowing as much as you do on the case by now. I'll tell you about this snafu when you get here. I'm downtown in the tank. If you can make it in twenty-four hours, I should still be here. Never know with these hotheads. All I can tell you now—but hurry—I'll make it worth your while if you spring me."

Worth my while? With all that was going on, I

should have been able to milk all the players for a fancy fee.

It was not a happy message for me. Apparently, the boys in blue had something on Rolf. If the cops solved the case, goodbye fee.

I put in a call to Sgt. Keith Wajahowski, the detective who suffered me, more or less.... He wasn't in. I left a message I was headed that way and would be greatly obliged if I could chat a few moments with him in re: prisoner Rolf Gorberg.

I passed Daddy Pimple on the way out. Wretched timing. He stopped dead in his tracks. Oh, if only he could have dropped dead instead. But not to be. Instead, he gave me his latest pick from his antique collection of witty putdowns:

"Going to do something to earn your pay for a change?"

I thought, at my salary, a one-armed paperhanger would be underpaid. I only smiled as though that was the funniest thing I'd ever heard. That was the thing about Daddybucks, Realtor Ass., all you had to do to pull his chain was to make believe you thought he was the funniest thing to ever come down the dirt road.

So I chuckled with the smile and said, as I passed, "What a wit!" I'm sure he didn't hear my amendment of the sentiment with the insertion of "half" in front of "wit."

By the time I made it downtown to cop haven and "the tank" as Rolf Gorberg so colorfully put it, Detective Keith Wajahowski had returned to his desk chair. As I wandered in, I saw the detective turning pages in a folder.

"Oh, hi, Gates," he said on seeing me without looking up. Must have gotten my message. "Your boy's been a baaad, baaad boy."

"What?"

"Caught him planting fake evidence in Bel Air—we're very sensitive about that here, Gates."

"Yates."

"Sure as shootin'!"

"What's he say?"

"The usual malarkey about it all being a gag. He'd taken his wife to visit her sister, Mrs. Jackson—you know, with the guns."

"Yeah."

"Jason Q. Jackson was not there. Rolf'd seen the guns—so when the girls are yakking in the kitchen, he helps himself to one and ferries it to his car. Numskull!"

"You already have the ballistics and know it's not the gun?"

"Bingo. Head of the class for you—Yates, is it?"

"Yes. What did he want?"

"'Just a gag,' he said." Wajahowski shook his head. "'S what makes this job such a snap sometimes. The perps are no Einsteins—"

"Do you have anything you can indict on? Anything that will hold water in court?"

Now Detective Wajahowski squinted at me, like maybe I was no Einstein, either. "We'll find it," he said. "Don't worry."

"Thanks," I said, standing. "He called to see me. If I get anything useful, I'll pass it on."

"I'm sure you will," he said, as though sure of the opposite.

Little did he know, finding this patsy Gorberg guilty would not make my twenty-four hour period. I saw my fee taking wings.

There's no describing the look of Rolf Gorberg as they brought him into the visiting room in the tank. Chagrin, embarrassment, mortification—everything but guilt. Maybe he'd been an auto mechanic before he latched onto the incredible Sampson wealth, but he'd left that behind at the altar of the kitsch, but quaint, Las Vegas chapel where the deed was done.

"This is a crazy mistake," he said, beseeching me with a restrained wave of his handcuffed hands. For a moment, I thought he was taking blame. I should have known better.

"Cops are clowns," he said. "Coming in on me like the mod squad."

"How did they know you were there?"

"Damned if I know—and they won't tell me. Obviously, someone snitched."

"Who would do that? Why?"

"Beats me."

"So what *were* you doing there?"

"Man, it was all a joke. I took the gun over there as a *joke*. Obviously, it wasn't the gun that was used."

"How do you know?"

"I just picked it up at random. The cops already checked Jason's guns and didn't find the one that matched the bullets that got Orville. I mean, my God, if I had done it, as they seem to suspect, why in the *world* would I go back there with the gun?"

"Maybe they think a guilty conscience drove you back."

"Oh, no way. I'm not guilty of anything! Well, a harmless prank, maybe."

I wondered if he were so naïve, and if he'd pull a similar prank at the airport metal detectors: "Oh, I just happen to be packing some heat, ha ha!"

Didn't seem likely.

"But what motivated you to pull this?"

"Don't know. Wasn't thinking, I guess." (He was no slouch at understatement.) "I just had visions of Jason looking for the gun for days and not finding it, then getting a call from Pamela saying, 'Come get your gun,' or 'Is this pistol yours?' You got to admit, there are some laughs there."

If there were, I didn't find them.

"Look, you got to get me out of here—"

"I'd like to help. I'm afraid I don't know how to go about it, unless you get a lawyer."

"I *hate* lawyers," he said. "But I got one working on it. Way they charge around here, I expect most of the work is done with calculators, figuring how best to screw you. Anyway, nothing is happening. Cops say no bail for murder one. Murder? Can you imagine?"

I could imagine, though I wasn't sure I could imagine the scenario here. I tried to shock Rolf. "Did you know Jason Q. Jackson shot up his first wife?"

I could tell by the slow processing of raw data in his cerebral computer that I'd surprised him.

"No! When? Where? Who? She die? I had a hunch it was him—"

"That's why you took his gun out there to the Sampson place?"

He shrugged. "Maybe. Maybe I thought the police needed a little prodding. A little pointing in the right direction."

I could see he was making it up to fit the circumstances. But he was such a creepy guy, I think he'd have had trouble convincing his mother.

"Yes, that's it," he was saying. "So why aren't they investigating Jason?"

I shrugged. "Maybe they are. Maybe they don't buy it."

"They got *me* in here, instead. I'm the *last* person that would have done this."

I made a gun with my fingers, pointed it at him and pulled the trigger.

"Yeah, well, *you* might have pulled the trigger. I didn't."

"But I never even *met* him."

"All I'm saying is, you are just as likely as me to have done it."

Not quite, I thought, but feewise, I hoped he was right.

TWENTY-SEVEN

BACK IN MY TRUSTY PLYMOUTH, I decided to head for Jason Q. Jackson's place. Check his reaction to the jailing of his brother-in-law, as well as my newfound knowledge about his itchy trigger finger vis-à-vis his ex. He certainly was back on my list of suspects, but then, all of them were. Maybe they were all in on it together, and all these latest developments arose from their attempt to shift the focus—make everyone look nuts.

Francine greeted me, though that may be too generous a description. Her expression hadn't changed—still down in the mouth, still that silent, wary look about her.

"Is Jason here?"

She shook her head.

"Oh. Know when he'll back?" I asked, but even as those words shot by my teeth, I thought, this may be a silver opportunity.

"Never know," she said, like she really never knew.

"Do you have a minute to talk to me?"

She gave me a once over with her wary eyes. "Why should I?"

"I bring some news—an update, perhaps, on my investigation."

She stepped aside. I walked into the living room. "May I sit?"

"Suit yourself," she said with a faux insouciance. I could tell she was curious.

"Did Jason ever tell you about his first wife?"

"Not much," she said, "just that she was crazy."

I looked at her with some astonishment. That's the American way, I thought, the victim is always crazy. "Did you know he shot her?"

"Shot her?" she said, as though trying to fit a pesky piece in a puzzle. "I don't believe it."

"I just talked to her." I made a head bowing gesture toward the gun cabinet. "Has a withered arm as a result."

"Why do you tell me this?"

I hesitated, I calculated. "Maybe so you'll be careful not to rile him—not to do anything that will make him think *you're* crazy. Or…" I made the gun gesture with my fingers again. She wasn't amused.

"I don't think," she said, then stopped to think. After she thought, she thought better of completing the sentence.

"Tell me, do you have a will?"

"A will? Me? Why?"

"The usual reason," I said, trying to make it sound unimportant.

"Which is?"

"Well, to pass your assets at the time of death to the person or persons you so designate."

"That would be my husband, of course," she said without much conviction. "Isn't there some law about it?"

"California has community property laws," I said. "A spouse is entitled to half the assets that were earned during the marriage. You are free to dispose of anything else the way you choose. The money you inherit is your sole separate property—you can do anything you want with it."

She looked dazed. Perhaps she was on some controlled substance. "Why are you telling me this?"

"I just thought if you are considering a will, what with your husband's history on the trigger, you might want to make a pointed effort to tell him he won't inherit the big pot."

"I'll keep that in mind," she said with smoldering resentment.

"You know about Rolf Gorberg?"

She nodded somberly. "Brenda called me all hysterical," she said. "I can't blame her, I guess. What was he thinking?"

"He tells me it was all a prank. For laughs. I don't think he's laughing," I said. "Was Rolf noted for his sense of humor?"

"Hardly."

"Any reason he'd frame Jason? Other than the obvious one, of course?"

"Getting us out of the will picture. I can't think of anything else."

"What's your take on Kurt Roberts?"

"I don't trust him."

"Jason—?"

"Doesn't trust him, either."

"Why not?"

"He's playing both sides against the middle. He encourages us to sue, then he drops out. Then he runs to tell Orville little Kurtie would never sue Big Daddy. Perish the thought!" She was piqued. "Of course, you know Kurt had an affair with Pamela."

"I'd heard some rumors. How does that affect the dynamics of this business?"

"Maybe he thought he could just off the old man, so what was the point of suing? At least Brenda and I were going through legal channels."

For some reason, when she said, "legal channels," I looked over at the glass-cased guns, and thought of all the *il*legal channels they portended.

"How did you feel about your father—really?"

She pondered the question. "Okay, I guess. He wasn't much of a father. That's a given, I guess. You don't make that kind of money babysitting and going to school plays."

"Did it hurt when he called you a drug addict?"

"Well, of *course* it hurt. After the suit, he couldn't wait to badmouth us. His corporate raider training, I suppose."

"Do you do any drugs?"

Her back stiffened. "I take some medication, yes, but I'm not a drug addict. I am *dependent,* yes, but that's a chemical condition in my body. That's the difference between being rich and poor. If you have enough money, you can get doctors to prescribe the *medicine.* You don't have to buy relief illicitly on the street."

Perhaps people who give information so freely often do it to mislead.

"But he's one to talk," she said. "The number of pills Orville took would sink a battleship. He imagined he had every disease known to man. When a new disease was discovered, he caught it right away." She shook her head.

"Who is his doctor?" I asked.

"Why?"

"Just thought I'd talk to him. He might have some insight into Orville's hypochondria."

She bought it. "Dr. Irving was his favorite," she said. "He had many."

"Did you know you have a half-sister in Mexico?"

"What?" She was startled.

"Do you know anything about his trips to Tecate?"

She shook her head, dumbfounded.

"The million he settled on his daughter before he died?"

She was still shaking her head. "When it came to the rest," she said, "I guess there was a lot we didn't know about the old man."

"Any idea where he could have put five hundred thou in cash?"

"Excuse me?"

"That's what I can't account for. He took one and a half million in cash out of the bank a couple months before he died. Arvilla got the mil—"

"Arvilla?"

"Sis." I laughed, and I shouldn't have. Francine wasn't amused. "I was just thinking of the similarities to Shakespeare's *King Lear* with Orville and you three daughters, when suddenly, there's a *fourth* daughter. It's like, what now, King Lear?"

I'm not sure Francine knew who King Lear was, or Shakespeare, for that matter, but, no matter. She said she had no idea about Orville's "financial shenanigans."

"All I know is, I got my monthly allowance."

"It didn't stop when he died?"

"No."

"Not even a blip?"

"Not even a blip. Kept coming as though nothing had happened."

"Good accounting," I said.

"Orville only hired the best," she said with, I

thought, a touch of pride. "Apparently it's a separate maintenance trust."

"So you'll never starve?"

She glared at me. I guess she didn't appreciate my observation: ten thou a month might be okay in some quarters, but here it paled next to three hundred million.

I heard a car drive up. I felt a moment of panic. It was one easy thing to tell Francine about her hubby shooting his ex-wife, and quite another to face him with it—especially with so many guns in evidence.

When I saw the smile with legs cross the threshold, I knew I'd made a mistake telling Francine about Smiley's marksmanship vis-à-vis the distaff. She was waiting for him. No sooner had he gotten the words, "Gil, how's it going?" out of his mouth, then she entered the fray.

"Jason! Gil tells me you shot your ex-wife!"

Jason shot me a look with deader aim than any of his high-powered rifles. "Where'd you hear that?" he asked, with understandable anger. It was an accusation, not a question, but, it must be admitted, not an answer, either. The smile never left his lips, though it faded somewhat.

"I met her," I said.

"You met who?" He was challenging me.

"Lucy."

"She's crazy, you know," he said. "Certifiable. Where'd you find her?"

"So you can finish the job?"

"So I can talk some sense into her. She has to stop spreading these lies."

"You didn't shoot her?"

"No, I didn't."

"What happened?"

"A gun went off—I don't even know how—"

"Could someone have pulled the trigger?"

"Bumped it. Hey, I'm not in jail, am I?"

"Don't seem to be."

"Think if anyone thought I shot her on purpose, I'd be running around like this?" he asked. "Hey your father helped me out of that mess."

"He did? How come I didn't know….?"

"Didn't want to worry your pretty head. It was nothing."

Since his smiling teeth were glittering with spittle like Frankenstein's monster, I decided against making a fuss. I simply shrugged as though it were nothing to me.

"Any idea why Rolf would want to plant your gun at the Sampson house?"

"He's nuts," he said. His assessments of others were taking on similar vibrations.

"That's it? Just a crazy, random act?"

"I can't explain it."

"Why not? You have any kind of run-in with him?"

"Can't figure it out. Maybe he thought with Pamela out in intensive care, he'd pull the stunt, hide the pistol, and hope the cops were so damn dumb they wouldn't bother to compare it to the bullets that killed Orville. Hell, they've already been through all my guns. It's just a desperation tactic. Rolf is *real* itchy to get his hands on that money, and, unless someone solves the case, he's out of luck." Then he added, as though it just came to him, "We all are."

"While we're on the subject, what do you make of Kurt and his dogs chewing up Pamela?"

"Kind of extreme way to do her in."

"To increase his share?"

"That, too."

"What else?"

"You know, they had an affair, those two—Kurt and Pamela."

"I imagine it's over…"

"Yeah, I'd say so. But this latest trick of his makes me think the two of them might have been in on it. He was afraid he was going to take the fall for it, so he took his puppies to shut her up."

"Any evidence?"

"Just a hunch."

"Kurt says it was accidental."

"Yeah." Jason smiled. "And I'm Bill Clinton."

Francine jumped in, "You'd better not be."

They both thought that a lot funnier than I did. "You have any idea about the Mexican thing with Orville?" I asked Jason.

"What Mexican thing?"

Francine answered, "Orville had a child. He gave her a million bucks before he died."

Jason seemed set back with the news. If I had any character judgment, I'd say he was legit. But I had swung from thinking none of them could have done it to any one of them could have—together, or in any combination.

Did any one of them, despite their protestations, know of the newly-discovered Mexican daughter? And might he, she or they have feared the million was just the beginning, and their shares would be diluted by twenty percent?

Not a solid motive for murder for most of us whose net worth is somewhat shy of three hundred million, but there is no accounting for greed.

TWENTY-EIGHT

I STARTED WITH the cancer specialist. The others were a urologist, internist, chiropractor, opthamologist, and neurologist. Why not? I thought, he could afford it.

Dr. Irving's digs were plush, indeed. Beverly Hills plush. If you had to succumb to the big C, Dr. Irving was going to see to it you went out in style.

I'd called ahead for an appointment, and, from the look of the place, I didn't think the doc would want to waste too much revenue-enhancing time on me.

But he was a cheerful sort. He ushered me in with a broad smile, and waved at an upholstered wing chair across his hand-carved rosewood desk. "Gil," he said, extending his hand, "Charlie—you wanted to talk about Orville Sampson—what can I tell you?" He shrugged as though that were a hopeless case. "A helluva nice guy. Can't imagine anyone wanting to give him a hangnail, much less murder him."

My eyebrows went upstairs. "Not even his kids—their husbands?"

He frowned. "I don't know them. Normal people I'm talking about. I'm not talking about freaks of nature who aren't satisfied with a gift of three hundred million."

"As a man of science, have you any idea how Orville got *three* of them? A hundred percent of the litter?"

He shook his head. "Genetic bad luck."

"So how was Orville's health?"

"Never as bad as he thought. I don't mean to disparage this prince among men, who treated his gardeners as well as he treats…well, me, or his banker, but Orville Sampson was a bit of a hypochondriac."

"What was his condition?"

"Pretty bad."

"Dying?"

"I'd say so. But we're all dying…at different rates."

"I'm reminded of the saying: 'Never murder a man who is committing suicide.' Why shoot a man who has terminal cancer?"

"Only if you didn't know it, I suppose, or believe it."

"Did Orville believe it?"

"Even before it was true," Dr. Irving said. "But, no matter what I told him, he always asked sheepishly if I would mind if he got another opinion."

"What did you say?"

"Not at all. I welcomed other opinions. Knowledge is more germane to our profession than ego."

"But he had cancer?"

"Ultimately, yes."

"Did all the other doctors agree?"

"With the diagnosis? Pretty much. Of course, if you look long enough and hard enough, you can find someone to say what you want to hear. Orville even went to Mexico for a Mexican miracle."

"When you say Orville thought he had cancer before he did, do you believe a person can will themselves to have a disease?"

"Worry, stress and anxiety can affect a person's physical condition. Whether or not stress can actually cause cancer, I don't believe it can. It can certainly weaken your resistance—affect your body's ability to fight it."

"What causes cancer?"

"I think it's largely genetic. Orville's mother died of cancer and so did his grandfather. That's as far back as he had any knowledge of family. He knew that. It worried him."

"He needn't have worried," I said. "As it turned out. How long do you think he had to live before he was shot?"

"I try not to play that guessing game, because I'm so often wrong. I'll give a guy six months and he lasts three years. Six months to a year will sometimes buy you five years."

"Did you tell Orville that?"

"Certainly."

"What other opinions did he get?"

"I think most were in the six months range—"

"When did he get those opinions?"

"He never *stopped* getting them."

"Did he share those opinions with you?"

"Oh, sometimes, but it was too much, really. I couldn't keep up."

"Do you know if he shared this info with anybody?"

"Not that I know of. He didn't want me telling anybody. I'd be surprised if he told the kids. The lawsuit was killing him and communication had come to a standstill, if Orville is to be believed."

"What about the daughter that didn't sue?"

"I don't think Orville trusted any of them. In fact, he had suspicions one of them would do him in."

"But his *wife?* Would he tell her his condition?"

"I think he might have, but, there again, she'd listened to so much doom and gloom from him, I doubt the cry of wolf would stir any passion in her. Why don't you ask her?"

"Thanks, I think I will. Anything else you can think of that might be helpful?"

He seemed to put some thought behind that accordianed brow. "You might start with the doctors who knew he was dying."

His secretary gave me the yellow pages.

TWENTY-NINE

IT WASN'T EASY chasing down all those doctors—would you believe twelve? With Dr. Irving, a baker's dozen. I was surprised Orville wasn't superstitious about the number.

I got more or less the same story from each—Orville usually exaggerated his condition, but this time he was on the money. How much time they gave him ranged from three to six months to two to three years. There seemed to be only one discernible pattern in these opinions: the later Orville went to the doctor, the shorter the estimate of remaining life.

But the surprising thing was none of them had ever spoken to any of Orville's children, or his wife. Most of the doctors thought it was somewhat unusual that no family member made any effort to discern the condition of a close relative. The consensus was, in addition to being a hypochondriac, Orville was secretive.

To my queries, "Did his wife know?" they all said, "Why don't you ask her?"

It was my next stop.

I couldn't drive up the long driveway in Bel Air

without thinking what a nice cemetery this place would make. Two gardeners were horsing with the lawn, mowing and edging, while another was shaving the miles of hedge with a grown up electric razor.

The door was opened crisply to my authoritative knock. There before me stood the quintessential British butler, large, bearlike, and correct. I was so taken aback, my first thought was Jeeves was hired, not from any butler agency, but from Central Casting. Could Pamela have moved? I'd never seen a butler here before.

"Has Pamela returned safely?"

"Pamela is quite safe," he said with an edge, as though I meant to harm her.

"May I see her, please? Gil Yates—"

He looked me over, not with disdain, perhaps, but without losing much love, either. "I shall tell Mrs. Sampson you are here. She does need her rest, and perhaps a few days more would be preferable."

I shot him a squinty eye. "Just tell her, please," I said with some umph behind it.

"One moment, sir." And he closed the door.

When he returned, his face showed he was bearing bad news. "Madam will see you," he said.

He led me to the master bedroom where "Madam" was sitting in a reclining chair with her legs horizontal on an ottoman—the bandages somewhat lighter, but still ubiquitous.

"Gil!"

"Glad to be home?"

"Am I? I'm glad to be alive."

"What's with Jeeves?" I asked, throwing a thumb over my shoulder in the direction of the nether world.

She gave a low chuckle. "Harvey," she said, "that's Harvey. He's a dear—"

"Beneath the stern visage beats a heart of gold?"

"You got it."

"Where'd he come from?"

"What? Oh, England. Can't you tell?"

"I don't know—lot of ersatz Britishers around nowadays. He wasn't here before?"

"Nonsense! He's been with us for, well, before my time, and that's over nine years now."

"I never saw…"

"Course not," she said. "I sent them home after…after the…ah, murder. They hadn't been home in years—wouldn't hear of leaving us—but I convinced them with Orville gone, I could easily manage. I'm a simple girl, really, I never was too comfy with all these servants. Orville never wanted me to have to do anything, and besides, he liked the feeling of opulence—like he could afford anything—and he jolly well could."

"Jolly well? Is that Harvey talk?"

"Oh, Gil, just a fun expression. I suppose Harvey uses it."

I had this crazy notion that Harvey had done the job because he was crazy in love with Pamela. Then made himself scarce. "Did the police interview Harvey before he left?"

"Oh, yes. They talked to everyone."

"All the employees?"

"Yes."

"Who else was there?"

"Harvey, the maid, Ophelia—that's Harvey's wife."

My jaw dropped. Made my instant theory more remote.

"Then there are the three gardeners. Now, it's Xavier, Diego, Ignacio, I believe. They come and go—"

"Where do they go?"

"Back to Mexico."

"Illegals?"

"Oh, I don't know. One of them has papers, I think. Maybe all, but they have family in Mexico, and they go back. So it isn't always the same three—most of the time it is, I think."

"Were these the same three who were here at the time of the murder?"

"Gosh, I don't know. Harvey would know. He's the major domo around here." I must have squinted, for she added, "No, Gil, it's not what you think. Harvey was loyal to a fault. I begged him to take time off. He obliged me reluctantly. He came running back when he heard what had happened to me. I mean, he was on the plane next day."

"Was his wife?"

"Ophelia? Of course. They're an inseparable team."

"Anyone else on the staff?"

"Not full-time."

"Part-time?"

"There is a cleaning crew. Jean Cleans," she said.

"How are the employees paid?"

"Orville had his accountant set up on automatic pay to their bank accounts. He wanted them to get the money as soon as possible without waiting for the erratic mail. He was so good to them," she said, stifling a sniffle.

"Do you have an alarm system?"

"Yes."

"Who knows the code to turn it off?"

"All the employees, I believe."

"The kids?"

She hesitated. "Kurt does," she said. "I'm not sure about the others."

"Any suspicions about anybody who works here?"

"Gosh, no. Orville loved his employees."

"It was reciprocal?"

"Lord, yes. He spoke in this atrocious Spanish to the gardeners, and he was so proud of it. I think they appreciated the effort he made. He spoke in nouns, mostly—verbless Spanish, he called it. The gardeners talked slowly and used simple words with him. Their English was better than his Spanish, but he wanted to *noblesse oblige* them."

"May I talk to them?"

"Sure."

"I could do the employees all at once—save time."

"Anything you want. Who knows? It could help with some leads. But I'll tell you this, none of those employees killed Orville. They were just too fond of him."

"You know Rolf is in the slammer for planting a gun of Jason's here."

She shook her head at the folly. "Crazy," she said.

Funny, I thought, Kurt said the same thing, and by this time I was beginning to agree: they were *all* crazy.

"May I ask about your relationship with Kurt Roberts?"

"You already did." She smiled, then followed it with a steam engine sigh. "We were…close," she said.

"How do you account for it?"

"Oh, how *can* you account for these things? Vulnerability, opportunity, proximity, timing. You decide. He's also a lot younger. I was flattered by his attentions."

"Could he have had ulterior motives?"

Her laugh was almost like a man's. "That boy doesn't *breathe* without ulterior motives."

"So what were his?"

"Oh, I suppose it might have been simple lust, but I don't think so. Not with Kurt. Ingratiating himself as close to the source of the funds as he could get. He'd ask a lot of money questions when my guard was down."

"Like what?"

"Oh, who was Orville's accountant, what I thought of him. Where did Orville bank locally? If I knew what his will was like."

"Did you?"

"No. If I did, I wouldn't have told him—well, maybe I would have—my head was light in those days."

"Did Orville know or suspect?"

"I doubt it. He was preoccupied with his own honeys."

"Did he know you knew that?"

"I expect he did."

"Think there's any chance Kurt wanted to get caught—to maybe get Orville angry enough to divorce you—or even cut you out of the will—which would fatten nicely Kurt and Lolly's share?"

"Before he sicked the dogs on me, I'd have gone to the mat arguing against that one. Now it seems obvious."

"So why did he try to kill you? Why now?"

"I don't have the answer. And don't look at me like that, I'm not hiding any case-breaking secret. Why would I hire you if I knew who did it?"

"If that's a serious question, I'll tell you what you must already know: to throw me off the scent. It isn't costing you anything, after all, to muddle the case because you have some culpability, or to get a fact or some truth out that, for some reason, you could not put forth with any credibility."

"Oh, my, I underestimated you."

"So, why the dog bites?" I asked, waving at her bandages.

"Well, it's not personal, I'm sure. In his twisted mind, he thought it would look like an accident. I wonder how many he could kill to boost his pocketbook. I should think he'd have to change his method—accidental dog bites wouldn't wash more than once."

"What are your feelings about the culprit?" I asked.

"My money is still on the boys—both Rolf and Kurt have certainly incriminated themselves."

"And Jason shot his ex-wife."

"What do you think, Gil?"

"I'm still looking," I said. "Not ready to commit. Lot of unusual factors to be considered."

"I'll say," she said, laying a hand on her bandaged thigh.

I didn't tell her I thought the kids were innocent. The stunts they pulled were just too irrational.

In response to my gentle prodding, Pamela Sampson said she would have Harvey set up a meeting with all the help on the morrow. She would call me with the time.

THIRTY

BEFORE I RETURNED for the meeting with Orville Sampson's beloved employees, I wrote down every scenario in every combination I could imagine. One idea led to another; each one could have made a story of its own.

I speculated on where we would meet and what that would tell me. Harvey, of course, would pick the locale, but would he choose to sully his own bailiwick with the presence of three dirty gardeners, or would he and his wife go slumming to some garden shed?

On arrival, I paid my respects to Pamela. She was in good humor and said the pain was still pesky, but subsiding.

"We've got to solve this thing, Gil," she said with a worried look on her face. "I'm afraid talking to the employees who worshipped Orville is a waste of time—not that I mean to interfere…"

"Of course not," I said, hoping it came out sincerely. "But you never know what you can learn from talking to people. And, since you set it up, and I'm here, why not?"

She waved me on and I went downstairs to meet a sturdy, cheery woman in the uniform of the household:

black dress, white apron. I was hoping for something less traditional, but Orville, being born and raised in dirt poor, hardscrabble Texas, must have, understandably, thought tradition was class and vice versa.

"Hello, I'm Ophelia." She smiled, unstinting of her round eyes and flattering, full lips. "Harvey's wife." She curtsied! "We're meeting out back," she said. "I'll show you the way."

We met in the perfect venue: a room attached to the house, and yet, not part of the house. It was large and occupied with serviceable furniture. There were chairs that might have belonged to a dining room set before a major redecoration, a table and a desk, to which Harvey had staked his claim.

He did stand up when I entered, but it may well have been for his wife, who deferentially came in behind me.

"Your pardon, sir," Harvey said. "I was just catching up on some paperwork. Would you like to sit here?"

"Oh, no, that's fine." I waved him back to his chair. So, this commodious room was his office.

"If you would allow me to introduce you, sir—you have met my wife, Ophelia." She did an encore on the curtsy. "The gardening staff, Mr. Yates. This is Xavier, the lead man, Diego, his brother, and Ignacio, their cousin."

I tried to take each one in as he was introduced. Diego and Xavier looked suitably humble and a little scared. Ignacio looked more the tough guy, more than a little put out by the gathering. He played the macho stud of the trio—the show-me guy.

"We have all talked to the police," Harvey said gratuitously, "and I believe all of us were asleep when Orville was killed."

Everyone nodded eagerly, except Ignacio, who was toughing it out.

"Ignacio," I said, "were you asleep?"

"*Sí*—in *México*."

With questions that put my Spanish to the test, and help from Harvey, who knew the score, I learned that Ignacio had gone back to Mexico at the time of the murder.

I soon discovered Xavier had the best English among the gardeners, though it was halting and thickly accented. He was the only one with papers, having been granddaddied in on the last amnesty—our benevolent government's face-saving *modus* for stanching the unstanchable flow of Mexicans into this country. Xavier told me, with no lack of pride, that the Mexicans did all the dirty work the gringos wouldn't touch. So, trying to keep out the Mexicans was a sham. California and Texas and not a few other places would come to a standstill without Mexican immigrants.

"Is very 'spensive for to come back," Xavier said.

"How expensive?" I asked.

"Twelve hundred dollars for coyote. Coyotes get rich because of American laws no one wants to enforce."

Ignacio apparently understood. "We come hidden in trunk of car. *Sin dignidad.*"

I nodded my sympathy. Apparently, they thought I was an agent of the government who might be able to do something about it. But, when you have a poor country next to a rich one, you can't keep the poor out. They will climb fences, dig tunnels, swim rivers, pay twelve hundred dollars (a year's wages in Mexico) to hide in the trunk of a car. And there are exponentially more coming in than our meager forces can keep out. It's like the drug war: unwinnable.

"Was anyone else working here when Orville was killed?"

Xavier looked at me as though he didn't understand.

"*¿Otro hombre trabajó aquí, cuando Orville Sampson se murió?*" I got as close as I could in Spanish. Still I got a blank from Xavier.

Harvey chimed in, "There was that other cousin, wasn't there? Substituting for Ignacio? His brother, wasn't he?"

Xavier's eyes wandered. He nodded slowly.

"*¿Cómo se llama?*" I asked. "What's his name?"

"Raphael," Xavier said.

"Ah, yes," Harvey said. "He wasn't here very long, was he?"

"*Tres semanas, no más,*" Xavier said. "*Un sustituto de Ignacio.*" (Three weeks, no more, he substituted for Ignacio.)

I don't know why, but I got the feeling neither Xavier nor Diego was comfortable with this meeting. Ignacio continued to smirk as though he were an Italian lover-boy on the make.

"You don't mean he paid twelve hundred dollars and was only here for three weeks. How could he afford that?"

It turned out he had been picking tomatoes in Oxnard, up the coast, and just came down to help out.

"Did he go back to pick tomatoes?"

"No sé," Xavier said. (He didn't know.)

"¿Ignacio? ¿Comprende? ¿Volvió Raphael a México, cuando volvió Usted al norte?" (Did Raphael return to Mexico when you returned north?)

"No sé." Ignacio shrugged.

"Do you know where he is now?" *(Ahora?)*

Ignacio shrugged. Not his brother's keeper, apparently.

"If I wanted to talk to him, how could I find him?" I asked.

Nobody seemed to know.

"Where did you send his last check?" I asked the boss.

"That's all handled by Orville's accountant," Harvey said. Then he added, "These workers come and go, based, I suppose, on the workload."

"Was there much work when Ignacio went to Mexico?"

Xavier seemed confused.

"What month was it? *¿Qué mes?*"

"*Enero,*" Harvey answered for Xavier. "January. In the rainy season they go home. Christmas, sometimes. Much less work in winter, wouldn't you say, Xavier?"

"*¿Menos trabajo en diciembre y enero?*" I helped.

"*Sí.*"

"Last Christmas, did you go home?"

He shook his head.

I looked at Diego. "*¿Volvió Usted a México para la navidad?*"

Diego shook his head, I thought, with a touch of guilt. Was he guilt-ridden for not paying tribute to his mother and father at Christmas, or for something else?

I asked the assembled employees what they thought of their late boss and the gardeners' eyes lit up like a Christmas special, or, rather, a *navidad especiale.*

"We all loved him," Harvey answered for them all. Everyone nodded their consent, even the recalcitrant Ignacio.

"And we flatter ourselves to think he loved us," Ophelia chimed in. I wondered if he loved Ophelia in the Biblical sense, given his propensities, but I couldn't decide.

"He was like a generous uncle to us," Xavier said. "I would have done anything for him."

Diego and Ignacio nodded their agreement.

"We never worked for anyone who treated us better."

I thanked them and told them I might return with

more questions. And if any of them thought of anything in the meantime that might help the case, I was prepared to give a ten thousand dollar reward to anyone who could give me what I needed to arrest the killer.

Surprisingly, no one perked up at that offer. Either they knew nothing, or it wasn't enough.

After the gardeners left, I had a word with Harvey. "You're in charge of the gardeners?"

"Yes, sir. In a way, that is."

"How's that?"

"I look to Xavier to run the crew—my responsibility would be to the overall picture."

"You don't hire and fire?"

"No, sir. Xavier sees to that. When one of them goes to Mexico, he supplies a substitute—as in the case of Raphael at the time of Mr. Sampson's death."

"Anything bother you about that?"

"No, sir," he said with a bristle, as though I were questioning his judgment.

"First, Orville died in January—correct?"

"Yes, sir."

"Low season for gardening."

"Yes, sir—" less enthusiastic, more fearful of what was coming.

"Time when most of them might return to Mexico?"

Harvey nodded. I could tell his gears were churning, they just weren't meshing, yet.

"So I have a couple questions. *Numero uno,* why would they need to fill Ignacio's place? Rainy season, less work. And *dos,* they claimed Raphael was picking tomatoes before he came here, but, by winter, the tomatoes are long gone."

"Perhaps he was picking something else. Citrus, for instance."

"They said tomatoes. They are experts at agriculture—the seasons and whatnot, yet they want me to believe tomato season was just ending and Raphael just came down from Oxnard in the interim. What do we know about Raphael?"

Harvey shrugged. "He's Ignacio's brother," he said as though that were a glowing testimonial.

"Did you have anything to do with him?"

"Not much. Xavier ran the crew, as I said."

"Weren't suspicious—adding another person for the rainy season?"

"No. Xavier wasn't above making work for a relative. Orville indulged him. Orville loved his garden and was willing to pay anything to keep it up. If Xavier had relatives between picking seasons who needed work, why, he gave it to them."

"And they came and went pretty much at Xavier's whim?"

"Pretty much, sir."

"And the bit about picking tomatoes in the wintertime didn't bother you?"

"No, sir. They do grow them in hothouses, you know. Or it could have been a language thing."

I thanked Harvey and Ophelia, and stopped by to see Pamela again on the way out.

"What did I tell you?" she said when I came in and made an empty-handed gesture. "They loved him. They would have done anything for him."

"So they said. So what do I have? *Nada*."

"*Nada?*"

"Means nothing."

"Nothing? With Kurt trying to kill me with his dogs and Rolf planting guns and Jason shooting his ex-wife, I should think you'd have plenty."

"Yeah, sure, take your pick of the loonies."

"I wouldn't be surprised if they were all in on it and are finally in a panic you'll discover it, so they are frantically trying to incriminate each other."

"Maybe," I said, "I'm keeping them in mind. In the meantime, before one or all confesses, how much sway do you have with Orville's accountant?"

"Zach Nunnally? He's good folks." She smiled an unthreatening smile in my direction. "Shouldn't we start referring to him as *my* accountant?"

"Touché," I said, "Exactly so. Since he is your accountant, here's what I'd like him to do…"

THIRTY-ONE

PAMELA SAMPSON, bless her, laid my needs on Zach Nunnaly, *her* accountant, and, being a man cognizant of the butter vis-à-vis the staff of life, he performed his tasks with the alacrity of a trained seal. With very little wheezing accompaniment.

My request for an audience was immediately granted, and there was no waiting on the outside. He had, per my request, checked the employees' bank accounts—not a dead pipe cinch, he assured me—but he had connections, and some startling revelations resulted from those checks.

Xavier, Diego and Ignacio each had one hundred thousand dollars and change in their accounts, all deposited on the same day. All in cash.

That accounted for three hundred of the five hundred g's of the missing cash.

Raphael, the substitute gardener, had no known bank account, and no social security number to check.

So, maybe those loving gardeners offed the old man for the cash. Would he have it lying around the house anywhere they could just pick it up? Would they know it? Orville was friendly, but I don't think he had been that foolhardy.

Zach Nunnaly agreed. "I can't see any reason for Orville to go to his gardeners and say, 'By the way, I have a half million in cash stashed up in my bedroom bureau drawer—top left with the socks."

"And I can't account for two hundred," I said. "But the funny thing is, even Ignacio got a hundred thousand and he wasn't around when Orville was shot."

"So you think Orville just wanted to be generous to the boys?"

"Was that precedented?"

"Not that I know of. Oh, some ladies came in for a nice piece of change, but never in those numbers."

"So what's the scenario? Beneficent Orville hands one hundred grand to each of his three gardeners—cash—lot cleaner with a couple of checks. A hundred grand each goes into three bank accounts, including the USA account of one of the boys who is in Mexico. Accounts which customarily held a few hundred dollars suddenly jump by one hundred thousand. The joint account of his beloved butler and maid—much longer in service than the gardeners—has not a blip."

"Well, he could have decided to reward them at different times. Or, maybe he gave Ophelia and Harvey the other two hundred thousand and they took it to England with them—deposited it 'at home'."

"That would make some sense," I said. "But if he

thought he was going to die, and wanted to give them the money, why not just will it to them?"

"Tax considerations, maybe. If he left five hundred thousand dollars in the estate, it would have been subject to a fifty-five percent federal tax. He was way over the six hundred and fifty thousand deduction. So, by giving them one hundred thousand in cash, he saved about two hundred and seventy-five thousand in taxes for his estate."

"Was Orville that sophisticated about taxes?"

"You better believe it," Zach said. "All that trouble with his kids came about from Orville trying to beat Uncle Sam and his IRS."

"Think it's a coincidence he is shot the day before this goes in the bank? And soon after the murder, Harvey and Ophelia sashay back to Merry Old England?"

"Coincidence? If it isn't, what does it mean? The people who loved him most decided to pop him off and just found a half mil lying around? Not too likely, I'd say. I think he took the money out expressly to give it to them. Ask Harvey if he got two hundred g's."

"He'll tell me the truth?"

"I have a feeling he will. Especially if you let him know you can trace the cash through the world bank system."

"Can I do that?"

"Maybe not, but if you don't know that, the chances are Harvey won't know it, either."

Back to the Bel Air manse of Pamela and the late Orville Sampson. The gardeners were raking the flower beds and pruning dead roses. Was it my imagination they looked at me with fear? A fear that I somehow shared their guilty secret? I waved happily back at them and I saw a couple of pained smiles. Ignacio ignored me.

I parked in the generous driveway and made my way to the door—my back to the toilers in the landscape. That, I'd hoped, would tip them off—since I was not afraid of them, there must be nothing for them to be afraid of. Ah, the convoluted thinking we ascribe to mere mortals.

My knock on the front door was answered by Harvey. "Oh," he said with a frown, "I'm afraid Madam is resting."

"That's all right, I came to talk to you—if I may."

He looked startled. Guiltily so. "Certainly, sir," he said, but he didn't move.

"Mind if I come in?"

"Oh, I don't know if that would be proper—without Madam's permission."

I gave him the fisheye. "Come, now, Harvey, we can go to your room out back. It won't take long."

"Then…" he began to say, "why not here—" but I waved him off.

"Sorry, not where the gardeners can hear."

He hesitated.

"Of course, if you want…Madam's permission, I will be happy to share my suspicions with her first."

"Suspicions?" He didn't like the word. "Very good, sir," he said, and I followed him to the back room. We passed Ophelia toiling at the kitchen butcher block chopping all manner of veggies.

"Oh, hi," she said with a friendly smile. Harvey shot her a look to hold the friendly bit.

"Hello, Ophelia," I said, "would you be able to join us for a minute? Won't take long."

She looked to her hubby for a sign and she got it. "Gee, I think not, thank you. I'm awfully busy."

"Oh, I think Mrs. Sampson would want you to co-operate." I gave her my friendliest smile.

"I…"

"If you wish, I will wait for her permission." I turned to Harvey. "Wasn't that the same offer I made you?"

"Come along, Ophelia," he said without fanfare.

This time, I sat at Harvey's desk without asking, and Ophelia turned a chair from the table to face me. Harvey stood, apparently piqued by my choice of a seat. "Please sit down," I said to Harvey. He frowned, hesitated, then sat.

"As you may know," I began, "the three permanent gardeners each put one hundred thousand dollars in cash into their bank accounts the day after Orville Sampson died."

Their astonished reactions—eyes exploding, jaws

agape, simultaneous exclamations of *"What?"*—led me to believe their reactions were genuine. I didn't think either of them was an accomplished actor of that caliber.

While Harvey knit his brow and Ophelia shook her head, I said, "That leaves two hundred thousand in cash he took out of the bank before he died unaccounted for." I let it sink in, but, apparently, it wasn't sinking. "So, the obvious question is, did you two get one hundred thousand each?"

Harvey seemed legitimately dumbfounded as he shook his head in a daze. Ophelia followed suit.

"Any idea why they would get the money if you didn't?"

The heads wagged again like zombies. Harvey seemed to be trying to sort it out. Ophelia was just out. Were they picturing one hundred thousand dollars with wings flying just out of their grasp? But if no one got it, and it was meant for Harvey and Ophelia, where was it?

"Maybe it's still in his room somewhere? Did he have a safe in the house?"

"Oh, no, sir—we've been all through the house."

"Looking for the money?"

"No, sir," he snapped. "We knew nothing about the money. We did as we thought we'd be expected. Tidy up his belongings."

"Did you take anything?"

"Oh, no, sir," he said, clearly affronted. "Madam

said I could have anything, but I wouldn't hear of it. I would not imagine myself worthy to wear his clothes, even if they fit, which they did not."

"Any money around? Trinkets? Jewelry?"

"Yes, sir. I turned it over to Madam. She wanted me to take his very expensive gold watch, but I just could not."

"Your wife agree?"

"Yes," he snapped. "Ophelia was in accord with my wishes."

I wasn't convinced, but I couldn't connect this line of questioning with anything helpful.

"You know," I said, playing my Queen, "I can have the cash traced through the International Bank Organization. So, if you got it, save us all the trouble—it's no disgrace if Orville wanted to give you one hundred thousand or two—nor is it illegal."

He looked right through me. I felt it on my spine. "We *didn't* get it. Look anywhere you want."

"Any late-breaking ideas on why your fellow employees would benefit so handsomely, when you didn't?"

His dazed look and the slight shifting of his head told the story. "No...I...No, I...don't," he said with an expression that said, "I'm not going to stop trying to understand it."

"Let me know if you figure anything out, will you?"

He nodded, but he wasn't there in anything but body.

"You too?" I said to Ophelia. She nodded.

"I'll tell you this," Harvey said. "I will bet my *life* those boys came by that money honestly."

"Even Ignacio?" I said. "Ignacio was in Mexico when the money went into his account."

"Maybe Orville put it there to surprise them. Maybe they don't even know it's there."

"Yes, yes, and butterflies give Pepsi Cola."

"Why don't you ask them if they know there's one hundred thousand dollars in their bank accounts?"

"Think they'll tell the truth?"

"I think you'll read it in their faces. They are good, God fearing people—not murderers or thieves."

"I'll check it out," I said.

THIRTY-TWO

I COLLECTED THE GARDENERS on Orville's beloved grass. It seemed fitting. Their nervousness seemed to have escalated ten-fold. Even macho Ignacio seemed a touch edgy.

When they were gathered around me, with their hang-dog looks, their feet pawing the turf, I said, "I know about the money." I just dropped it there at their dancing feet.

Nobody said, "What money?" Nobody even looked up.

What now, King Lear?

"Want to tell me about it?"

Xavier spoke for the group—reluctantly. He combined his English with some Spanish. His compadres understood very little English, and I think he was being considerate.

"Orville wanted us to have the money," he said.

"He gave it to you?"

"Yes."

"Cash?"

"Yes."

"Why?"

"If he weren't dead, you could ask him."

"I'm asking you. You're still alive." I tried to boost my tone with a little threat.

Xavier shrugged. "He liked us."

"And fish have jet engines."

"He often did nice things…"

"One hundred thousand dollars nice?"

Xavier shrugged, checking out his brother and cousin in the process. Their long faces didn't vary. "Orville was dying."

"He told you that?"

"Yes."

"But, you know, he always thought he was dying."

Xavier closed his eyes and shook his head. "This time…real."

"How do you know?"

"I know. That's all I can say."

I heard some rustling. I looked up and saw Pamela hobbling toward us with the help of a cane. "What's up, Gil?" she said, looking askance at our huddle, like I might have been wasting their time with some nonsense, questioning those she knew were innocent.

She stood there, leaning with both hands on the cane, listening intently.

I filled her in on our conversation to that moment. She expressed silent surprise.

"So he gave you the money as a bequest?" I questioned Xavier. "A farewell present?"

He closed his eyes and nodded again.

I could feel their feet twisting on the grass without taking my eyes off their faces. Xavier in the center, flanked on my left by Diego, and my right by Ignacio. They seemed to gravitate closer together, as though drawn by some invisible magnetic force, closer with each question.

"Nice gift," I said.

"*Muy,*" he said. "Orville was a wonderful man."

"So why did someone kill him?"

Xavier's eyes shifted to his compadres. "Tell him," Diego whispered hoarsely.

"No!" Ignacio exclaimed with a force that startled all of us.

"Shall I call the police?" I talked tough. Ignacio answered me with a menacing look. "Or *imigración?*"

"*Tell* him," Diego said in Spanish. "We only did what he asked."

"*¡i imposible!*" Ignacio shouted.

Xavier shook his head. "We protect Orville. It is what he wanted."

"Okay, don't tell me. I'll tell you. Only, correct me if I'm wrong. Otherwise, you don't have to say anything.

"Ignacio went to Mexico for Christmas, to see his family. But it was really to get someone to do the job—to kill Orville."

Diego was beginning to tear up.

"I suspect it was a brother—or a close relative he could trust. You boys each took one hundred g's. The hit man got two hundred. Fair enough, I suppose. Right so far?"

None of them spoke.

"I suppose, out of the two hundred thousand, he had to produce the gun and the silencer, so the household would not be aroused. And he succeeded. Neither Pamela, Harvey nor Ophelia heard anything. It was a cinch for you to get in, you knew how to disarm the alarm system."

"Oh, Gil," Pamela said, "you don't seriously think…"

I held my hand up to her. Didn't she notice no one was protesting?

"I'm going to let you boys tell me how you got the money. I have my theory. I'll tell you if you're right."

Xavier tried to bluff, "I told you, he gave it to us."

"Why? What did you do for a half million dollars?"

Xavier's lips tightened. Diego blurted out, "Raphael shot him! He paid to have Raphael shoot him—"

I translated the Spanish to English for Pamela. I thought the top of her head was going to blow off.

"Orville said he was dying and he didn't want to suffer any more. He called it a mercy killing. Said we were Dr. Kervorkovich."

"Kevorkian," I corrected him. Pamela was tearing up, but a rueful smile crossed her lips.

Xavier took it from there. "Is true," he said reluctantly. Telling the tale gave no pleasure. "Orville said he had fixed his will so no one would get any money. He said no one gave him any money, and his wife and kids would be well taken care of, but if no one could solve the mystery—my cousin Raphael was back in Mexico—we each had one hundred thousand not to talk, then no one could get his money. He said it was too much money. So much money was a burden. His children took him to court. That killed him, he said. A bullet would just make it official. He only asked us to do it while he was sleeping and not to tell him when it was going to happen. And not to tell anyone because as long as the 'crime' was not solved, nobody would get his money."

The boys all had tears in their eyes. So did Pamela. Xavier sniffled. "I guess now Orville won't get his wish."

I looked at Pamela. She shook her head as if trying to clear it. "I don't know, Gil," she said. "My memory is not what it used to be. I'm having a lot of trouble remembering what I just heard. I'm so lousy at Spanish. I do remember telling you I didn't need any more money—and I meant it. How's your memory?" she asked.

"How's my memory?" I repeated her words with cloudy eyes. "I don't remember. I used to have a memory, but I plumb forgot it."

We looked at each other, the five of us exchanging knowing glances and our tears turned to broadening smiles as we hugged each other and Pamela's cane fell to the grass.

When I stooped down to pick up Pamela's cane, I thought of that stoop Rolf Gorberg and how he was mistakenly still in jail.

"You think we should make some effort to spring Rolf from the slammer?" I asked.

"Oh," she said, turning her nose, "I suppose that would be the cricket thing to do—sooner or later, don't you?"

"I suppose," I said, "but sooner or later the police will realize he didn't do anything more than acting stupid, and they'll let him go."

"Perhaps we shouldn't interfere with the orderly wheels of justice," she said. "My sons-in-law deserve each other, far as I can see." I couldn't argue. "They pulled the craziest stunts to rile each other."

As we walked back to the house, Pamela said, "Your fee, Gil…"

She had read my mind. I shrugged. What could I say? I'd laid down those specific layers of what I would earn with arrest and indictment, conviction, execution, and I knew, technically, I had met none of them. But I didn't think I would rock the canoe. My principal was satisfied with the result, and if I wanted to be ethical about it, that was all that should matter.

"I guess I talked myself out of it—since you won't be getting the inheritance."

"Now, Gil, do you think I would do that to you? A guy with eyes as blue as you've got?"

"Well, I was hoping for some honorarium."

"Honorarium, nonsense. I've got a well-stocked bank account. Orville saw to that before he hired that Hispanic Kevorkian."

"You knew?"

"No, no, I didn't *know*. But I think Orville knew for sure he was going, because I got quite a nice bundle. More than I'll ever need. I don't have kids and I'm not leaving it to *his* kids against his wishes."

"Good for you."

"Why don't you come inside," she said with a wink. "See if I can satisfy you?"

And she did.

HARLEQUIN®
INTRIGUE®
WE'LL LEAVE YOU BREATHLESS!

If you've been looking for thrilling tales of
contemporary passion and sensuous love stories
with taut, edge-of-the-seat suspense—then
you'll love Harlequin Intrigue!

Every month, you'll meet six new heroes
who are guaranteed to make your spine tingle
and your pulse pound. With them you'll enter
into the exciting world of Harlequin Intrigue—
where your life is on the line
and so is your heart!

THAT'S INTRIGUE—
ROMANTIC SUSPENSE
AT ITS BEST!

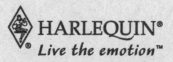